# LET IT BE ME

## MEN OF THE MISFIT INN BOOK #1

### KAIT NOLAN

TAKE THE LEAP PUBLISHING

**Let It Be Me**

Written and published by Kait Nolan

Cover design by Najla Qamber

Copyright © 2020 by Kait Nolan

All rights reserved.

AUTHOR'S NOTE: The following is a work of fiction. All people, places, and events are purely products of the author's imagination. Any resemblance to actual people, places, or events is entirely coincidental.

*For Amy, narrator extraordinaire,*
*Thank you for giving life to all the people in my head*

# A LETTER TO READERS

Dear Reader,

This book is set in the Deep South. As such, it contains a great deal of colorful, colloquial, and occasionally grammatically incorrect language. This is a deliberate choice on my part as an author to most accurately represent the region where I have lived my entire life. This book also contains swearing and pre-marital sex between the lead couple, as those things are part of the realistic lives of characters of this generation, and of many of my readers.

If any of these things are not your cup of tea, please consider that you may not be the right audience for this book. There are scores of other books out there that are written with you in mind. In fact, I've got a list of some of my favorite authors who write on the sweeter side on my website at https://kaitnolan.com/on-the-sweeter-side/

If you choose to stick with me, I hope you enjoy!

Happy reading!

Kait

# CHAPTER 1

"*I* am not drunk enough for this."

As truly horrific honky-tonk music slammed into her like a freight train, Emerson wished for a shot of something stout and the silence of the recording booth. Emerson almost turned around to go home to Hamilton as the blonde on stage reached the ear-splitting chorus of "Stand By Your Man." But her boyfriend had blown their plans tonight because of work, and she'd promised Paisley she'd meet her new man. It seemed a shame to waste all the effort she'd put into her appearance for the cancelled date, so she'd dragged herself all the way into Nashville to Lower Broadway.

Weaving her way through the crowd that didn't seem in the least deterred by the steady drizzle of spring rain, Emerson scanned the bar for familiar brunette curls. As she edged past too many bodies, her phone vibrated. Fishing it out, she saw *Fiona Gaffney* flash across the screen. Her goddaughter. One of the lights of her life. It was too damned loud to answer now. She'd get this meet and greet over with and call her back on the way home.

"Emmy!" Paisley's excited squeal reached her, even over the

catcalling toward the stage. She materialized out of the throng and looped an arm through Emerson's. "You came!"

"You did *not* tell me it was karaoke night. You know how I feel about karaoke." She had to lean close to be heard over the noise. Bad music aside, Paisley knew she avoided places like this because she had to protect her voice for work.

But her long-time friend didn't wilt under the accusatory stare. "Oh, don't be a fuddy duddy." She began to drag Emerson through the bar. "You *need* to hear Dustin sing."

"Please tell me you haven't latched on to another country music hopeful." Her excessively romantic best friend had definitely had a type back in college. They'd attended more than their fair share of open mic nights and karaoke competitions in the name of being supportive.

"God no. He's just got a gorgeous voice." Paisley winked. "And a really great ass."

Stopping at a high-top table with a sandy-haired guy in jeans and an untucked black button down, she waved an enthusiastic hand. "Dustin, baby, this is my dearest, darling bestie, Emerson Aldridge. Emerson, my boyfriend, Dustin Phelps."

Emerson shook his proffered hand and slid onto one of the chairs, sending up a prayer of sincere gratitude as the caterwauling from the stage finally stopped. Why? Why couldn't they have picked one of the other venues that had actual *good* music? There were so many to choose from.

Once the waitress had taken her order, Dustin leaned across the table. "So Emerson, what is it you do?"

Yet again she had to lean too close to be heard without shouting. "I'm a voice actor."

"Yeah? Like, what? Cartoons? Video games?"

"Sometimes. But mostly I do audiobooks."

He blinked. "So you read for a living."

She performed entire casts of characters, giving unique voices to each, such that listeners had a well-rounded experience and felt immersed in the story. But sure. They could just reduce her life's work down to reading. He clearly wasn't an audiobook listener. A lot of people didn't understand, and she was not in the proper mood to educate him, particularly as she suspected he wouldn't last the month once Paisley had her fill.

"I suppose."

Did he even know that Paisley wrote romance? If he didn't, how serious could this relationship be?

*One drink.* She'd have one drink and visit for a bit, then the social niceties would be discharged and she could go back home to the quiet. As the next pair of singers took the stage for an extremely drunk rendition of "Beer Run," she knew that would be sooner rather than later. She was absolutely not in the mood for this. But she did her best to engage in conversation during the lulls between singers, listening to Dustin talk about his job as assistant baseball coach for one of the area universities. That explained the nice ass. Nearly a dozen more tone-deaf performers took the stage, each progressively worse than the last. Emerson wondered if blood was leaking from her ears. Where the hell was her drink?

Paisley studied her face. "You are not in a fun-loving-Emerson frame of mind."

She definitely was not. But that wasn't Paisley's fault, and it wasn't fair of her to spoil the night. Reeling in her lousy mood, she offered an apologetic smile. "I'm sorry. I'm disappointed that Blaine's work schedule ruined what was supposed to be a romantic date night. Again. I know he's trying to make partner, but I'm feeling a bit neglected lately." The past few months, he'd been so dialed into work. At first, she'd been fine with it. It had given her time to really dig in and expand her own portfolio, making her name known in the industry. But she missed coming out like this with him. Being third wheel was not what she'd had in mind for tonight.

"That sucks. But it's all the more reason to come out with girl-friends!"

Emerson slid a look over to Dustin, who was scrolling on his phone.

Paisley leaned closer. "Okay, fair point. But we haven't gotten together in forever. I feel like I never see you anymore since you started dating Blaine."

The waitress finally came back with her drink, and Emerson pounced on it in the name of buying herself time to find an answer. She *had* let her friendship slide in the past year since Blaine had come into her life. To some extent that was to be expected with a new relationship, but she could absolutely make more of an effort.

Before she could say as much, she spotted another familiar face across the room and froze.

Surely it wasn't him.

But even as she watched, Blaine laughed and loosed that megawatt grin she'd seen him whip out at countless meet-and-greet mixers for work. What the hell was he doing at a karaoke bar on Lower Broadway? This wasn't the kind of networking his firm engaged in. His arm was around the shoulders of another woman. The same one in cling-wrap jeans who'd been butchering Tammy Wynette when Emerson came in.

Paisley followed her gaze. "Is that...Oh shit."

Blaine hauled the blonde to her toes and planted a smoldering kiss on her mouth.

Emerson was out of her seat and walking over before she could think better of it. She had to be sure. She dodged around tables, circling the room until she came up behind him. He still had his mouth fused to the blonde when she tapped on his shoulder.

His head came up, and the utter shock on his face was all the answer she needed. "Emerson?"

"You had to work?" How many times had he used that excuse

and been doing this?

Blaine released the blonde, opening his mouth to make some kind of an explanation, but Emerson just lifted a trembling hand. "Don't bother. We're done."

She needed to get the hell out of here before the reaction set in because, right now, she wasn't sure if she'd fall apart or utterly lose her shit, and she wasn't keen on having an audience for either. Eye on the door, she turned.

"Emerson, wait." Blaine caught her by the arm and jerked her around.

She led with the drink still in her hand, flinging it in his face. "Let me go, you cheating bastard!"

He released her, howling as the alcohol dripped into his eyes. "What the hell!"

Taking advantage of his momentary blindness, she hustled back to the table to grab her purse. Dustin was throwing down some bills, and Paisley was gathering her own things.

"Don't bother. I'm sorry. I'm going home."

"But Emerson—"

"Seriously. Y'all stay and enjoy your date. Don't let me ruin your night, too." Not waiting for an answer, she pushed through the throng, dimly registering a few "You go girl"s from some of the women on her way to the door.

Outside, she stopped just underneath the awning, sucking in huge breaths of air.

Blaine was cheating on her. And if he was doing it now, he'd probably done it before. She'd made it so damned easy on him, with her homebody tendencies, so often focused on her work, on the books she loved. Content in her little house outside the city proper, away from all the lights, the traffic, the noise. The pressure of all of it pressed in on her as she trudged through the rain back to where she'd left her car. How much had changed in an hour.

She'd been a damned fool.

Her phone began to vibrate again.

If that son of a bitch was going to try to offer excuses, she'd just have to give him a piece of her mind. But the vitriol died on her tongue as she saw Fiona's name again.

She could hold it together long enough to talk to her. Hell, maybe talking to Fi would keep her distracted and calm until she got home and could fall apart in private.

"Hey honey. I'm sorry I missed your call earlier, I—"

"Is this Emerson Aldridge?" The deep, male voice was so unexpected, she pulled the phone away from her ear to check the display again.

"Yes?" Delayed concern began to set in, sharpening her tone. "Who is this? Where is Fiona?"

"I'm afraid there's been an accident."

* * *

AN INSTANT.

That was all it took for lives to be changed. Lives to be lost.

Caleb Romero knew that better than many. Had lived through that knife's edge when others had not. So he knew, before he even fully registered the truck barreling through the red light, before he heard the crash and shriek of metal, that someone else's life was over.

He slammed on his brakes, skidding a little on the rain-slicked pavement as he yanked his truck to the shoulder of the road. His mind was already assessing the scene as he leapt out, raced over. Other vehicles were stopping. Someone else would dial 911. He needed to check for survivors, start stabilization if he could.

The truck was flipped on its side, front end accordioned where it had struck the little sedan. The car... Jesus God. It was upside down, the driver's side entirely caved in. He didn't need to see past the blood on the shattered window to know the driver was likely a lost cause.

"Mom?"

The tremulous voice had his blood running cold.

His mind tried to throw him back to high school. Back to his own trauma. Caleb blanked it out, focusing instead on the here and now and the life still to be saved. He raced around to the passenger side, hunkering low to see through what remained of the window.

The girl hung upside down from the seatbelt, her blonde hair brushing the collapsed roof of the car. She reached out toward the woman dangling beside her in the driver's seat.

"Mom!"

"Hey. Hey there. I'm here to help."

Tears clogged her voice. "Help my mom."

It was more than evident, now that he could see, that her mother was beyond help. But now wasn't the time to bring that point home to the kid.

"More help is on the way." The distant wail of a siren underscored the point. "I need you to focus on me just now. Can you move? Are you hurt?"

The girl turned her head to look at him. Stiffly but with what appeared to be more or less full range of motion. "I don't...I..."

"Take it slow. Can you wiggle your fingers and toes?"

"Y...yes."

Good sign. "Are you having any severe pain anywhere?"

"I don't know. I don't think so."

She was definitely in shock, so no guarantees, but she didn't show any obvious signs of spinal injury. "Okay. We're gonna get you out of there."

Stripping off his jacket, Caleb used it to break out the last of the window, clearing a space. He didn't even ask if she could unbuckle the belt, just pulled out his pocket knife and carefully sliced through it, managing to catch her before she crashed to the ceiling of the car.

"I've gotcha." Carefully, he eased her out, not taking a full breath until her legs cleared the wreckage. His mind ran through triage. No signs of massive bleeding or breaks. But there could still be internal bleeding.

"She's dead, isn't she?"

The soft question stopped Caleb's assessment. He met the girl's shattered eyes, read the horror of knowledge, and swallowed as he felt the long ago echoes of his own. "I'm so sorry."

As sirens shrieked and emergency personnel began to swarm the scene, the girl slumped against him and wept.

She was the only survivor.

Because he knew what it was to be alone and terrified, Caleb had come with her to the hospital, done what needed doing. As a firefighter, he was a first responder and the emergency staff at this hospital knew him, so nobody kicked up a fuss.

By now, the tears had stopped, replaced by the glassy-eyed anesthesia of shock. After what she'd been through, that was a blessing, one that would end far too soon.

As Dr. Chahal performed the exam, the girl—Fiona—offered monosyllabic answers. Caleb wasn't sure she really heard anything the kind-eyed doctor said. He could feel the tremors wracking her slim frame through the hand gripping his like a vise. He remembered all too clearly how fear and grief pooled just below the surface, waiting to rise and strike. How, when the bubble burst, they'd all but torn him apart when he'd been barely older than she was.

Fiona Gaffney would have a hard, hard road. She'd need solid support. Caleb wondered if the godmother she'd had him call would be that for her.

In the end, Liya Chahal sat back, addressing him, though she kept her dark eyes on Fiona. "She's banged up, has some bruises and cuts from flying glass. But all in all, she's physically remarkably unharmed."

That was something, at least.

"Will she be cleared to leave?"

"Medically, yes."

They both knew there'd be legal paperwork to hash out in terms of who the girl would be allowed to leave with. Who knew how long that would take?

A nurse knocked on the door before slipping inside. "There's someone at the front desk pitching a fit to get back here for Miss Gaffney. An Emerson Aldridge?"

The hand holding Caleb's tightened as Fiona jolted upright. "Auntie Em?" She started to scramble off the bed.

"Hold it." Gently, Caleb pressed her back. "You stay put."

"But—"

"I'll bring her to you." There were things he needed to tell the woman before she got back here. Things he hadn't felt comfortable getting into over the phone with a traumatized fourteen-year-old listening in.

Fiona's eyes skittered to their joined hands.

Caleb squeezed, hoping she found the touch reassuring. "We'll be right back. I promise."

"I'll stay," the nurse offered. The entire emergency department already knew what they were dealing with here. News traveled fast.

After a long moment, Fiona's grip loosened, and Caleb slipped out of the room. On the way through the familiar labyrinth of hallways, he braced himself for what was coming. It didn't matter how many times he'd had to do it, these notifications never got any easier.

A water-logged woman stood at the triage desk, her hands white-knuckling the edge as she clearly struggled not to scream at the nurse on duty. "I was told she's here. I need to see her."

"Ma'am, as I said, if you're not family—"

"How many times do I have to tell you? Her father is not involved. I'm her godmother. I *am* the next closest thing to family."

"Emerson Aldridge?"

The woman whipped her head around at the sound of Caleb's voice. The carefully rehearsed words bled out of his brain as panicked blue eyes met his. The relative chaos of the waiting room faded away as he fell into those eyes, soaking up the sense of recognition, even though he knew he'd never seen her before.

*It's you.*

Startled by his own thought, he snapped out of his stupor and closed the distance and nodded to the nurse. "I've got this, Janette."

"Where's Fiona?"

"I'll take you to her. C'mon." He gestured toward the double doors, and she hustled toward them. "I'm Caleb Romero—the one who called you. You need to know right off that Fiona is okay. Minor injuries." It was the only comfort he'd be able to offer her tonight.

A little of the terror etched on her face faded as they pushed through the doors. But Emerson was sharp. "Could you not reach her mother?"

This was the part he hadn't wanted to tell her over the phone. Navigating her into one of the empty rooms off to the side, he shut the door. Emerson didn't move toward any of the chairs. Her whole body drew taut, and he recognized that, deep down, she already knew what was coming.

Tunneling a hand through his hair, Caleb sighed. "Fiona's mother was in the car. She didn't make it."

Like a puppet with suddenly cut strings, Emerson collapsed. It was instinct to catch her, to pull her against his body, as if he could somehow offer protection from the truth. She sucked in a ragged breath, and he waited for the scream of rage and pain. But she didn't make a sound as she wilted into him, her hands curled to ineffectual fists against his chest. Her silent, potent grief swamped them both for long minutes. Caleb felt a little like a voyeur. He didn't know this woman. But he knew this pain. So he held her, until she found the strength to stand again.

"You were there?" The question rasped out, as if her vocal cords had been torched.

"I saw it happen. I pulled Fiona out. There wasn't—" He stopped himself. The driver's side of the car had taken the brunt of the impact. She didn't need that horror in her head. "Her mom was already gone."

Emerson closed her eyes, absorbing that. Maybe she'd take comfort in the fact that death had been all but instant.

"Thank you for saving Fi." Her throat worked as she swallowed. "Does she know?"

"Yes."

She visibly armored up, pulling herself together for the sake of the child in a way that impressed the hell out of him. As she straightened, she seemed to register she was still pressed against him. A faint tinge of embarrassment brought color back to her pale cheeks.

Caleb forced himself to drop his arms and step back. "Are you up to seeing her now?"

She sucked in a breath and squared her shoulders. "Take me to her."

The moment they stepped through the door to the room, Fiona broke. Emerson didn't hesitate, edging onto the bed and pulling the girl tight into her arms as she sobbed, even as tears tracked down her own cheeks.

Eventually, the unintelligible cries turned into words. "I don't want to go to my grandparents. You know what they're like."

Emerson's face went fierce. "Not a chance in hell, baby. Your..." She swallowed. "Your mom made provisions. You're with me."

Everything in her posture and expression said she'd go to war for this kid.

Some tension in Caleb released. They had a long road to go, but he had a feeling these two would be just fine.

# CHAPTER 2

**4 Years Later**

*E*merson braced her hands on the kitchen counter and summoned every ounce of Mom-sternness she could manage. "Child, you have *got to pack.*"

Fiona swiped a Coke out of the fridge and shrugged with a nonchalance that had Emerson's blood pressure rising. "Eh."

She was a good kid. A great one, in fact. At no point during the dreaded high school years had she given Emerson more than a few silver hairs, and those had readily been dealt with by her stylist. There'd been no worrisome brushes with boys, no drinking, no excessive partying, and she'd been an exceptional student, all of which Emerson was eternally grateful for. But this whole college thing just might be the death of her. Or Fiona. She wasn't sure which.

Tamping down her frustration, she trailed her goddaughter down the hall, past the dining room that had been turned into a staging area, full of neatly ordered—by Emerson—piles of bedding, towels, bathroom gear, a microwave, shoe pockets and other detritus associated with freshman living, all packed, labeled, and ready to go. By contrast, the upstairs bedroom Fi swung into looked like a bomb had gone off. She had yet to pack any clothes or toiletries or the personal pictures and knickknacks that were a mark of home. Emerson didn't know if this was typical teenage procrastination or a sign of Fiona's true reluctance to go off to college.

She worried about that. Despite the fact that the kid could've gone out for Best Teen of the Year at any point, worry about Fi had been Emerson's default state since she became guardian to her best friend's child. Every day had been joy and grief as she saw Micah's eyes looking back at her. She'd done right by her goddaughter, fulfilling to the best of her ability the promise she'd made senior year of high school, when Fiona had been born and Micah's parents had disowned her. But she'd never stopped questioning whether it was enough, whether she'd gotten it right.

Pinching the bridge of her nose, Emerson sent up a prayer. *Micah, give me patience for our girl.* "Fiona."

Fi flopped into the lipstick-pink moon chair that was one of the few surfaces in the room not currently draped with clothes. "There's time."

"Honey, move-in day is *tomorrow.*" It wasn't as if she was ready for the girl to move out. A part of Emerson still wanted to wrap her in cotton and shield her from the world. But facts were facts. This was happening. All the paperwork was signed, the scholarship awarded. Fiona Elizabeth Gaffney was matriculating as a freshman tomorrow.

Thick, gold lashes hid her eyes as she shrugged again. "Yeah, but I'd rather spend the time with you. It's our last night together."

Twin surges of love and frustration shot through Emerson. She'd made Fi the center of her world. It was what they'd both needed. But moments like this, she wondered if she'd gone too far in that direction. Had they become codependent? Had she hobbled Fiona's natural progression to independence? Was she pushing her baby bird out of the nest too soon?

Whatever response she might have made was interrupted by a familiar knock on the back door. Fiona brightened, shooting out of her room like a rocket and bouncing past Emerson to fly downstairs.

She sighed. There'd be no packing now.

The low rumble of a male voice reached her before she got to the kitchen. Pausing in the hall to steel herself for the encounter, she called herself an idiot.

*It's just Caleb.*

Caleb Romero, their neighbor and resident hero, had become a familiar fixture over the years. In the weeks after the accident, he'd come by to check on them both. He'd been an unexpected anchor during turbulent times, at first helping out with things like the yard or picking up groceries, when they were both too overwhelmed to manage. Then he'd stuck around, popping over to drag them out to a movie or ball game, making sure they got out and lived a little.

When the house next door had gone up for sale, he'd bought it. And somehow he'd become a regular part of their lives. Over time, Fi's hero worship had evolved to something somewhere between friend, brother, and crush. And Emerson...well, she'd developed an improbable friendship with the younger man. If she objectively recognized he could stand in for a great many of the romance heroes she narrated, she was blaming it on the day job. And his six-pack abs. It didn't mean anything but that she appreciated God's sense of the artistic. He was way too young for her.

But that didn't stop her hormones from standing up and dancing a jig when he flashed that familiar grin in her direction as she came into the kitchen. Those double-barrel dimples had landed him as Mr. January in the local firefighter's calendar the last two years running. "Hey, Em."

"Hey." She resisted the urge to fan herself and grabbed a bottle of water from the fridge instead. "What brings you by this lovely August evening?"

He held up a gift bag. "I brought a dorm-warming gift for the graduate."

Emerson's heart turned to goo, even as Fiona made grabby hands.

"Oooo! Thank you! Gimme!"

Laughing, Caleb handed the bag over.

"Can I open it now?"

"Sure." He kicked back against the counter beside Emerson, crossing his arms over his chest. She averted her eyes so as not to gawk at how the gesture emphasized his pecs. As if she didn't know.

Fiona pulled a square plastic thing out of tissue paper, angling her head to read the label. "A microwave bacon tray?"

"I know how much you love bacon. Seems a shame to miss out on it in the dorm."

Laughing, she bounced over and gave him a side hug. "Thank you. That was really thoughtful. And you should totally stay for dinner tonight."

Emerson nearly choked on her water. Not that they didn't hang with him on the regular, but she usually had prior notice to prepare herself.

"You're not on duty until tomorrow morning, right?" Fiona pressed.

Because, of course, they knew Caleb's work schedule at the fire station. That was just neighborly. They watered plants and kept an eye out for mail and packages when he was on shift.

"I'm not, but I thought y'all were having girls' night." Those dark, chocolate eyes flicked to Emerson, and she could swear the temperature cranked up five degrees. "I wouldn't want to crash."

*It's just a hot flash. You're getting older.*

"You never crash," Fi assured him. "Besides, Emerson's just going to make me pack."

Exasperated she crossed her arms. "I'm still going to make you pack. Paisley will be here to load up *in the morning.*"

"It's only an hour away."

After all these years, did the child not understand how much Emerson needed to plan things? *"In the morning, child!"*

Fiona rolled out her lip in a pout. "You're just going to hang over me. You know I hate that."

Emerson did know, and she'd bent over backwards to walk the line between giving Fiona freedom and the structure she needed. But she'd had weeks to take care of this on her own. It hadn't happened. Emerson did *not* want to get to the point of loading their cars tomorrow and not be ready to go. It was August, for heaven's sake. The later in the day, the worse the oppressive heat and humidity would be.

Caleb's knowing gaze bounced between the two of them. "Okay, okay." He swung a brotherly arm around Fiona's shoulders. "I'll tell you what. Emerson needs a run. I'll get her out of your hair so you can pack in peace. And *if* you're actually done when we get back, I'll stick around and even spring for pizza."

"Excuse me?"

Both of them ignored her. When had they wrested all control of the situation from her hands?

Fi pursed her lips in calculation. "Emiliano's?"

Caleb's face twisted with mock offense that she dared to suggest he'd think of anywhere else. "Obviously."

The little minx stuck out a hand. "Deal."

They shook on it, and Fi headed back upstairs, presumably to get started.

Emerson stared at him. "Did you seriously just manage to bribe my child with pizza to do the thing I've been trying to get her to do for weeks?"

He flashed the grin again, dimples carving into his cheeks. "And my charming company, the value of which can't be overestimated."

Her lips twitched. He spoke nothing less than the truth. "Naturally."

It wasn't what she'd planned, but maybe this was better. With Caleb around for the night, there'd be no chance for the mood to devolve into somberness and tears. As Fiona had said. She was only going to be an hour away. This wasn't the end of everything.

She shoved away from the counter. "I'll go get changed."

"Meet you out front in ten."

* * *

"It's a girl!"

Phone pressed to his ear, Caleb stopped dead in his kitchen at his brother Porter's exclamation. "Wait, the baby's here? Isn't that early?"

"Two weeks. But she's fine. Maggie's fine. Everybody's healthy. Six pounds, five ounces. Born just a couple hours ago. We're naming her Faith Reynolds. She's got this soft downy hair and looks just like her mama."

"I'm an uncle." Caleb tunneled a hand through his hair and whooped. "I'm an uncle! Man, congratulations! You gotta send pictures."

"I will. I gotta get back, but I wanted to let you know."

"Yeah, of course. My love to Maggie." He signed off, practically dancing his way through changing his clothes.

The phone call from Porter delayed him enough that Emerson was already limbering up at the end of the driveway between their houses by the time he came out. He couldn't quite decide whether to curse his brother or buy him a beer as he took in those toned, tanned limbs exposed by the fitted tank and running shorts as she bent over to touch her toes.

*Stop checking her out, you asshole. She's stressed.*

Caleb could see it in the set of Emerson's shoulders and the restless flex of her muscles as she straightened up. Fiona moving out was a Big Deal. They all knew it, but Emerson hadn't talked about it. Not with him anyway. He hadn't pressed, but he knew it was weighing on her. This was the best method he'd found for draining off some of her anxiety.

"Porter's wife had the baby."

"Yeah? What'd they have?"

"Girl. Faith Reynolds Ingram. Six pounds five ounces. Porter sounds over the moon."

"As he should. I know these last several months with Maggie on bed rest had him freaked out."

"Everybody's healthy and safe."

"Have you figured out how to make yourself favorite uncle yet?"

Caleb rolled his own shoulders. "I'm sure it'll come to me. Ready?"

In answer, she pushed into a jog. He fell in, easily matching her pace as they headed up the road for their usual trail that led through the woods on the back side of the park. The four-mile loop was thick with trees and circled around the lake. Beneath the shade of the canopy, temperatures dipped into a more comfortable range. Well accustomed to Emerson's habits, he kept his mouth shut for the first mile. She had to find her stride and pound out some of that frustration before she unfolded enough to talk.

By the time they hit the lake, her breath had leveled and the tension had begun to melt out of her posture.

"Feel better?"

She shot him a glance that was somewhere between amused and annoyed. "Always do when you drag me out here."

It was why he'd prodded her into it years ago, but he'd never imagined they'd become regular running buddies back then. He'd never imagined a lot of things when he popped over to her house after that night at the hospital. In the beginning, he'd only wanted to do what he could to help that brutal transition for her and Fiona. After his own parents had been killed in similar fashion, there'd been no Emerson for him. He'd gone into foster care for his last few years before eighteen, winning the foster mom lottery in Joan Reynolds. She'd been the reason he'd gotten through the devastation, and a part of him had just wanted to pay it forward. But then he'd kept showing up, kept being pulled in by them both, and the admiration he'd felt for Emerson had deepened to more.

"There's something patently unfair about it," she continued, pulling his attention back to the present.

"Unfair about what?"

"The fact that it's hard, sweaty exercise that releases all the stress instead of a big ass bowl of ice cream."

Caleb could think of plenty of hot, sweaty things he'd like to do with her. Not that she seemed to have a clue about the less than gentlemanly thoughts he regularly entertained about her. He'd gone out of his way to hide them, hadn't he? He was pretty sure she'd relegated him to some kind of little brother status. Or she wanted to. He'd caught her ogling him when she thought he wasn't looking. He'd even done a fair amount of yardwork and outdoor home improvement projects shirtless, just to test the theory. Yeah. Emerson noticed him in a totally not-brother way.

He'd take it. That knowledge had kept him going these past four years, as he bided his time, being the friend he knew she needed, even as he yearned for more. She'd be shocked at how much more. With Fiona moving out, into the next phase of her life, Emerson would finally have the bandwidth to think about something other than the child she'd upended her life to raise. Which meant it was time to do something about shifting himself out of the Friend Zone.

He dragged his brain back to their conversation as he dropped back to let some other runners pass in the opposite direction. "Pretty sure it has something to do with endorphins and completing the stress response."

"I suppose I should be grateful. All this running means my ass didn't grow three sizes with all the ice cream and chocolate I've been stress eating since I became a parent."

Well that just made him look at her ass. All toned and shapely, it bounced just a little with her stride. His hands itched to cup it, kneading the muscles as he devoured her mouth.

*Down boy.*

Running a quick mental inventory of everything in the apparatus bay at the fire station, he picked up the pace, drawing even with her on the path again. Time to get to the real reason he'd brought her out here. "How are you doing with all this really?"

"I'm...I don't know. Worried." She laughed a little. "I mean, when am I not? But excited, too. I'm looking forward to some time alone." The moment the words fell out of her mouth, Emerson's face twisted in guilt and shame. "Don't get me wrong. I adore her. I just...it'll be nice not to be needed for a little while."

Caleb hoped she'd take the opportunity to explore her own needs, and that she'd let him be the one to fulfill them. "You're allowed to be relieved that your kid is growing up and getting out of the house. Maybe especially since you inherited one rather than making the choice for yourself."

Emerson shook her head. "I don't regret her for a moment. Just how I got her."

"I know."

For a moment, they both slid back to that rainy night. He knew she'd give anything to have Micah back. Did she think about how her life would've been different if there'd been no accident? If she hadn't suddenly been thrust into parenthood under horrific circumstances? He did. Would she have come into his life at all without the tragic beginning?

"Did you want kids before Fi?" He'd never asked her.

"In that sort of vague, someday kind of way. With the right guy."

"Do you still want kids?" It wasn't a deal breaker for him. He was legitimately curious.

Her glance said, *Please.* "I'm thirty-six and single. That ship has sailed."

"Plenty of people have kids later in life. Or there's always adoption."

She gave a noncommittal grunt. "Moot question at this point. I do *not* want to do the single parent thing again. Right now I just want to enjoy getting some of *me* back."

"Totally fair." He planned to be majorly instrumental in that process.

"What about you?"

Caleb blinked. "What about me?"

"Do you want kids?"

Did he? Like her, he had a sort of vague notion of them. But he hadn't thought much about kids the past few years. He'd just been thinking about her.

"With the right woman. If she wanted them."

Emerson smirked. "How's the search for her going?"

*Already found her. She just doesn't know it yet.*

"Eh, there's time."

"You sound like Fi." Her tone was full of exasperated affection.

"She's a great kid."

"She is."

They finished their circle of the lake, jogging back into the trees at a longer, more relaxed stride than they'd started.

"Do you think she's actually packing?"

"She loves Emiliano's, so yes." He felt certain of that. "Whether she's finished is another matter."

"Wanna take bets?"

"What are the stakes?"

"Winner buys cheesecake."

He knew exactly how much Emerson loved her cheesecake. "Deal."

By tacit agreement, they lapsed into silence and picked up their pace for the rest of the run. At the end of it, Emerson's cheeks were flushed and wisps of her honey-brown hair curled in a sweaty halo around her head. The lines of strain around her mouth were gone. Mission accomplished.

They trooped inside for water to find Fi proudly gesturing to a pile of bags and what appeared to be every laundry basket in the house.

"See? Packed."

"I didn't realize laundry baskets counted as luggage," Caleb observed.

Fiona grinned. "Only the finest. Besides, you set the terms and you said nothing about the *kind* of packing. I met my end of the agreement. Now you hold up yours. Emiliano's, my good man."

"Fair enough. I'll call it in."

Emerson moved toward the stairs. "I'm going to shower."

They both watched as she disappeared to the second floor. With a quick glance back, Fiona towed him into the kitchen.

"How is she?"

Caleb resisted the urge to smile. Neither of them knew how often he ended up being the go-between to check on the other. "Anxious. How are you?"

She nibbled at the edge of her thumb, a sure sign of her own anxiety. "Worried about how Emerson's going to do without me."

Telling her Em was relieved to be getting some time to herself might wreck something, so Caleb took a different tack. "I think she'll settle when you settle."

"I need you to do something for me."

Recognizing her tactics, he qualified, "If I can."

She laid out what she wanted. Caleb listened, nodding, asking questions here and there. It wasn't a half bad plan, as plans went, but he wasn't at all sure how Emerson would feel.

"Just take her. Let her decide when she gets there. Promise?"

"Promise what?" Emerson strolled back into the room, wet hair scraped back into a braid, her face freshly scrubbed and glowing.

"Extra spicy sausage," Fiona sang out.

"As long as there are peppers for me."

Caleb pressed a hand to his heart. "I feel like my pizza-ordering skills are being impugned here that either of you thinks I would forget your favorite toppings."

"We would never," Emerson assured him, ducking back into the fridge for another water.

*Promise,* Fiona mouthed.

In answer, he tapped his heart again. He'd do everything he could to take care of Emerson.

Meanwhile, he was ordering some pizza.

# CHAPTER 3

*P*eople milled everywhere and midday heat baked Emerson where she stood with Fiona and Paisley outside Richmond Hall. The cars had been emptied, all the boxes and bags and laundry baskets of stuff hauled up to the dorm. Fiona's bed had been made up with bright new bedding, the curtains had been hung, the drawers had been lined, and Fi was officially kicking them out.

"Seriously, I want to unpack myself."

Emerson thought of the mountain of stuff in the floor of room 317. "Are you sure you don't want help?"

"I'm a big girl. I can take care of it."

Emerson hoped that meant she really would put things away instead of living in chaos. The room wasn't that big, and she was having to share it. "But what about Lacey?"

"We'll *both* be unpacking. It'll be a bonding experience." She made shooing motions. "Scoot. I'll be fine."

Paisley swung an arm around Emerson's shoulders. "Our work here is done. C'mon, Mom."

Emerson repressed the *But* hovering on her tongue and opened her arms for a hug. Fiona didn't hesitate, wrapping tight around her. Emerson couldn't stop herself from turning her face into Fi's hair and breathing in the scent of her jasmine shampoo. "I can't believe you're in college. The next thing I know, you're gonna get married and be having kids of your own."

"Nah. I'm not having kids."

"Oh?"

"I can't possibly live up to the example you set. I love you, Em."

The child couldn't possibly know what it meant to her to hear that validation. Feeling watery, she squeezed tighter and swallowed against that pull in her throat. "I love you, sweetpea."

"I'll keep in touch. Promise. And you'll see me soon. I'm only an hour away, remember?"

"Right. Of course." She swallowed back the tears that wanted to fall.

Fiona stepped back. "I'm gonna go be a freshman and shit."

Emerson opened her mouth to correct the language but Paisley started laughing and waved her off. "Bye kid!"

With a happy bounce and a final wave goodbye, Fiona joined the stream of people heading into the dorms. They watched the doors for a few long moments before Paisley said, "So? Lunch?"

Emerson rubbed at the tension in her temples. "Can there be alcohol?"

"Shenanigans it is."

An hour later, the pair of them were ensconced in one of the dark leather booths at Emerson's favorite bar. Modeled after old-school Irish pubs, the place was full of dark wood, leather, and character. But the menu had a decidedly Southern slant, with cuisine that was a sort of Cajun-Irish fusion, honoring the heritage of owner and chef, Heath Brousseau. Heath himself was a treat for the ears, with his rich, rolling accent that could as easily switch from Cajun French profanities to an Irish lilt. He delivered their lunch himself, sliding the steaming plates in front of them.

"Where's our darlin' Fi?"

Wrapping both hands around her bottle of cider, Emerson

aimed for a smile. "We just moved her into the dorms."

"Ah." Heath nodded knowingly. "Allow me to send you a second round, on the house."

She grimaced. "Do I look that bad?"

"*Mais non.* But I figure it's appropriate, whether you're mourning or celebrating." His teeth flashed white. "Enjoy your lunch."

Bending over, she sucked in a deep breath of spicy boudin sausage and garlic mashed potatoes—not something she could usually indulge in at lunch if she was recording. The microphone she used was too sensitive to digestion noises. But she'd cleared the decks for today and tomorrow. "Mmm."

Paisley cut into her more classic fish and chips. "So, what are you going to do with your newfound freedom?"

Emerson sliced into her meal, forking up a bite of sausage and potatoes before slouching back in her seat and considering. "I'm going to sit in absolute silence. Have a bubble bath. Binge on the last four years of shows I haven't had time to watch because I had a talky teenager. Eat all the Indian and Thai food I want—extra spicy. And sleep in." They were pleasures she'd taken for granted before she'd become a parent. She wasn't about to do that again. This go round, she was going to *wallow* and *savor* all of it.

"Yeah, and after tomorrow?"

She didn't want to admit she couldn't quite see past tomorrow. "I figure that will keep me busy for a while."

Both brows winged up. "Honey, that is just sad. What about your love life?"

"What love life?" Her lady parts were so neglected, there might be cobwebs down there.

"Exactly! You should get one. I know you needed to focus on Fiona in the beginning, but you didn't have to cut yourself off from men entirely."

"I wasn't in any hurry to get back out there after Blaine." She didn't have it in her to go through the whole dating routine only to be disappointed again. And the last thing she'd wanted to do was introduce Fiona to some guy, let her get attached, only to have him turn out to be another asshole.

"That whole thing was shitty, absolutely. But it's been four years. Not all guys are douchecanoes. Case in point, the gorgeous hunk of a firefighter next door."

If all guys were like Caleb, maybe she'd have a different opinion on the matter. Dependable, trustworthy, supportive. Definite romance hero fodder.

"Yes, Caleb is a sweetheart, but we're just friends."

Paisley waggled her eyebrows. "Don't have to be."

The absurdity of that idea had her barking a laugh. "Don't be ridiculous. He's too young for me."

"Is he closer in age to you than Fiona?"

"Barely." Eight years younger was hardly close. For God's sake, he'd been in elementary school when she'd graduated high school.

"Barely is good enough. He is *hot*."

A fact which Emerson spent a great deal of energy and effort trying to ignore. Not easy with his propensity to run without a shirt. But she'd found a happy medium of being able to objectively appreciate his…attributes…without objectifying *him*. Most of the time.

"I do have eyes. That doesn't change the fact that I am not going to mack on my much younger neighbor. I value his friendship too much. It would make things super weird between us." She couldn't stand the thought of losing him as a friend, and she wouldn't do anything to upset his relationship with Fiona.

"I'm just sayin'," Paisley waved her longneck for emphasis, "if I were single and lived next door to *that*, I'd be doing something about it."

Paisley loved men. Loved dating. She considered her lengthy list of past relationships research for her romance novels. For Emerson, the very idea of serial dating, enjoying men for as long as she felt like before moving on to the next, sounded exhausting.

She hadn't had that much to put into *one* guy before Fiona. She sure didn't have the energy now.

"I'm not you." But now that Paisley had put the image into her head, Emerson couldn't quite stop herself from imagining that slow, sexy grin of Caleb's—the one he pulled out for the firefighter calendar—aimed at her. Heat pooled in her cheeks...and lower.

She took a long pull of cider, hoping to cool off. "I'm not looking for a guy, right now. I'm looking for myself."

Paisley lost the teasing edge to her smile, shifting to concern. "What do you mean?"

"It's part of being a parent. I came to it late in the game and in one of the most brutal ways possible. There was no guidebook or training for how to suddenly be the mom of a teenager. I've poured *everything* into making sure Fiona was okay—or as okay as she could be."

"You've been an absolute rockstar of a parent under incredibly challenging circumstances. I know you gave up a lot."

Emerson shook her head. "I don't know that I did. I try to remember what I wanted out of life before her, and I just...can't." In her mind, life was marked by that stark dividing line—Before The Accident and After The Accident. Before was incredibly fuzzy these days. "I don't regret it, and I don't resent her for it. God knows, she didn't ask for this either. But I don't remember who I am apart from her now. And I've only had her for four years. I can't imagine what moms feel when they've raised a child from birth."

"We have friends with kids. You and I both know how hard they have to work to maintain a sense of self outside the role of Mom. Maybe you slid over the line there because of the extenuating circumstances. But now is absolutely the time to fix that. Figure out who you are as a woman, not just a parent. I just think that a guy to remind you that you are attractive and vibrant and interesting would help with that."

And they were back to this again.

Paisley meant well. Emerson knew that. But the idea of having to be attractive and vibrant and interesting felt so insurmountably exhausting, she just couldn't think about it yet. Maybe after she'd had some time to adjust to her empty nest.

"Can we talk about something else?"

After another long, searching look, Paisley let the subject drop. "Fine. Let's talk about work. I should have the final edits done and a script ready for you next week. Are we still on for the first of the month?"

* * *

AFTER HIS FORTY-EIGHT-HOUR shift turned into more like sixty, Caleb was dreaming of a shower, a beer—maybe simultaneously— and eight straight on a horizontal surface. But he wanted to check in on Emerson first and find out how move-in day went. Was she enjoying the solitude like she thought she would? Or was the whole thing hitting her harder than she expected?

After indulging in that beer in the shower and scraping off what felt like four layers of soot and grime, he'd picked up her favorite ice cream and wine on the way home. Without even stopping at his own house, he crossed the span of lawn to Emerson's. The *ON AIR* sign she used to notify visitors and delivery personnel that she was in the recording booth and not to ring the bell was unlit, so he circled around the back to knock.

She didn't answer. Maybe she wasn't home. Or maybe she was indulging in a long soak in the tub. His brain had a quick little fantasy about bubbles and slick skin and a bathtub big enough for two before he reeled it back in. He tested the knob. Unlocked. Probably home, then. After a moment's hesitation he decided to slip into the kitchen, shove the ice cream in the freezer and leave the wine on the counter with a quick note.

The moment he opened the door, he heard the crying. The

exhaustion faded as he bolted toward the living room with all the situational readiness of a five-alarm fire. Emerson lay on the sofa, curled into a ball, sobbing. Dozens of wadded tissues surrounded her, and his brain clicked through, assessing. No blood. No sign of physical trauma.

"Emerson."

She shrieked, bolting upright at the sight of him.

"Sorry!" Lifting his hands in apology, he crouched in front of her. "Are you hurt?"

She shook her head and slumped again, grabbing another tissue to blow her nose.

Caleb let out a slow, controlled exhale, thinking he might need some of the wine himself to counteract the adrenaline dump. Scrubbing both hands over his still damp hair, he spotted the photo album that had slipped to the floor. Gently, he picked it up. He expected shots of Emerson and Fiona, but it was a different smiling face with Fiona's eyes. Her mom, Micah?

"She should have been here for this," Emerson rasped. "She would have been so proud."

A fresh spate of tears spilled over, and she dropped her face into her hands.

Heart twisting, Caleb set the album aside and sank down beside her on the sofa, reaching to pull her in. He didn't know if she'd let him. Physical affection wasn't something they did. But after only a moment's hesitation, she melted into him, the same way she had that night at the hospital. She wasn't silent now. Here was the storm he'd expected all those years ago. He wasn't under any delusion that she hadn't grieved the loss of her friend, but he wondered if some of this had been held off all this time because her focus was always forward, always on Fiona. It sounded like something Emerson would do.

She felt so small and fragile, shaking in his arms. So unlike the woman who rolled up her sleeves and waded in to do what needed doing. When was the last time she'd let herself just break down? Had she at all? Saying nothing, he held on, stroking her hair and down her spine, over and over, until the tears slowed and her body went limp with exhaustion.

He expected her to immediately shove away, but she stayed right where she was, tucked up against his chest, breathing softly. Had she fallen asleep? Not that he was complaining. He liked the feel of her in his arms, liked the sense of trust that she hadn't tried to stuff all that emotion away when he'd showed up. At least, he hoped it was trust.

"I soaked your shirt." Her soft voice was ragged.

"It'll dry," he murmured. "Do you want to talk about it?"

She shook her head and sat up, wiping at her face as she pulled away. "Why are you here?"

He itched to pull her back in but reached for the bag he'd brought instead. "I wanted to check on you. I came prepared to either celebrate"— He held up the Malbec—"or commiserate." He pulled out the Moose Tracks ice cream, which had started to melt.

Her blue eyes glimmered, and for a moment he thought she might cry again. She swallowed. "That was really sweet. Thank you."

"Which one would you like?"

Her lips twitched into a ghost of her usual smile. "Both?"

"That can be arranged." Caleb shoved up from the sofa and strode into the kitchen.

Knowing she'd want a few minutes to pull herself together, he took his time, digging in the utensil drawer for the corkscrew and ice cream scoop. Water ran in the bathroom down the hall as he opened the wine and began to fill two bowls with ice cream. Snagging one of the trays she kept for parties, he loaded up the ice cream, along with an empty wine glass, a bottle of ibuprofen, and a tall glass of ice water. She needed to rehydrate some before she started in on that wine. By the time he carried the tray into the living room, she'd adiosed all the tissues and washed her face.

At the sight of the tray, she crossed her arms. "Two bowls?"

Studiously not looking at how those arms emphasized her breasts in that tank top, he settled his cargo on the coffee table and handed her the water and medication. "It's my delivery fee. C'mon. Bottoms up."

As she swallowed it down, he dropped back onto the sofa and grabbed the remote, turning on the TV and flipping to Netflix.

"What are you doing?"

"Starting *Stranger Things*. I know you've been wanting to watch it. Why, did you want to watch something else?"

"You don't have to babysit me, Caleb."

As the unmistakable theme music began to play, he set the remote aside and settled back with his ice cream. "Are you kidding? Do you know how long I've been waiting to discuss this with you? Fiona doesn't know what she's missing by refusing to watch it. This show is *perfection* in television."

"You just surfaced from a forty-eight-hour shift."

"It wasn't a bad one." She didn't need to know about the overtime.

Emerson gave him the side eye. If she'd looked uncomfortable or like she really wanted him to go, he would've. But she needed to think about something else, and he was here to deliver—even if it wasn't the kind of distraction he might've preferred. Besides, it would be fun revisiting the eighties with someone who'd lived through it. Probably best not to mention that, though.

Reaching for her bowl, he handed it to her. "Eat your ice cream, Aldridge."

Folding herself onto the sofa beside him, she dug in, turning her attention to the screen. By the time the second episode started, she'd long since finished the ice cream and a glass of the wine, and he knew she was hooked. Without taking her eyes off the TV, she held out a hand, "Pass the wine."

Smiling, Caleb topped off her glass and settled in for a solid binge session.

# CHAPTER 4

*a* nagging throb in Emerson's skull pulled her from the most delicious dream about...what? Even as she reached for it, the pieces slid away, leaving her with nothing but the hangover. This. This was why she didn't indulge in crying jags. Or was it the wine? She'd lost count of how much she'd drunk. Surely Caleb hadn't let her finish the whole bottle by herself. She shifted her head to press her face into the pillow, hoping to block out the light. It wasn't morning until she said it was morning.

The pillow didn't give. It was hard and warm and...moved.

Shock banished the last traces of sleep as she realized her pillow was a muscular chest. Her whole body was plastered against the full length of a big, tall someone who shouldn't have fit on her sofa.

Oh dear God in heaven, she'd spent the night with Caleb on her couch.

What the hell was he still *doing* here?

Thinking hard, she unearthed a dim memory of finishing off the ice cream at two in the morning. She'd gotten cold, so he'd wrapped her up in a throw blanket and they'd...cuddled?

No. That couldn't be right. The cuddling was probably part of the dream because it had been so damned long since she'd been held. Paisley would no doubt have plenty to say about how sad that was. Not that Emerson needed reminding. She was so very aware that there'd been no one for her since Fiona became a daily part of her life.

But...here they were. Her leg was thrown over his muscled thigh, her arm was draped over his waist, and the only thing keeping her from crashing to the floor were the strong arms tucking her close enough she could feel his every inhalation against her breasts.

He felt so damned *good,* all wrapped around her. Solid and warm and safe. Everything in her wanted to burrow in and hold on to this feeling that, for just a little while, she wasn't standing alone.

Last night, she hadn't been. For the first time in what seemed like forever, she'd had someone share her grief. It should've been weird. But he'd been there the night everything changed. He understood, as no one else could, how much it had gutted her. She'd never shown anyone else, not even Fiona. That child had enough on her plate navigating her own grief.

It definitely wasn't grief she felt now as she breathed in Caleb's scent—that curious, intimate smell of sleep-warmed skin. She wanted to bury her nose against his throat and wiggle even closer. Not that she did any such thing. Moving would wake him up and then this was going to get really weird. She just wanted to enjoy the closeness for a little while longer.

And, yeah, okay, she wanted to catalog the sensation of being up close and personal with a body like his because holy hell. She spent so much time trying not to think about his physique. But there was no ignoring it now. Not when she could feel the ridges of those abs beneath her palm and the evidence of morning just brushing her thigh. Her long starved libido sat up and said, *Hello, Sailor!*

She should *not* be having these thoughts about Caleb

Romero. He was nearly a decade younger, for Pete's sake. She was not a cradle robber. But it was hard to think about cradles when all the evidence pressed against her pointed to a very, very adult body.

That body tensed in a long stretch, accompanied by a rusty groan that had all kinds of inappropriate thoughts sparking in her brain. Thoughts that weren't at all helped by the big hand that stroked down her waist, over her hip. Emerson couldn't decide whether she wanted him to settle that palm over the curve of her ass or not. Would it be worse to know how that felt or be left to imagine it?

He blinked open dark, devastating eyes and smiled. "Morning."

"Hi." *Brilliant conversation, Emerson. Way to be articulate.*

Should she move? She should move.

Caleb brushed the hair back from her face, lighting little fires where his fingers skimmed over her cheek. "Sleep okay?"

"I...uh..." How could she think with him so close? What was this look on his face? This wasn't easy, friendly, funny Caleb. This was...something else. Something had shifted between them, and Emerson didn't know what the hell to do with it.

"Why did you stay?" *Oh, great. Just blurt it out, why don't you?* But she needed to know.

"Because you asked me to."

*Oh God.*

Heat flooded her cheeks. After all his kindness last night, after the mess he'd walked in on, she'd *asked him to stay?*

Needing some distance, she started to shove up and away, but he just pulled her back, until she was sprawled fully atop him, chest to chest, his hands laced at the small of her back.

"And because I wanted to."

From her position, it was *very* obvious he meant it. Blatant interest shone in his eyes, which was befuddling and flattering and...so ridiculous. He was twenty-eight years old and in his absolute prime. She was in her mid-thirties, just realizing that she wasn't going to get back the life she'd put on hold to raise a child. There was no rewind, no do-over button.

"It was late. You were probably exhausted after your shift." In a bit of a panic, she pushed away, narrowly avoiding unmanning him as he let her go. This wasn't happening. It wasn't. It was just Paisley's stupid suggestion worming its way into her stupid skull.

Caleb straightened, and she chanced a look in his direction. No sign of offense or disappointment on his face. Those beautiful, sensual lips were twisted in...amusement. Damn him. And now she was looking at his mouth.

Jerking her gaze away, she smoothed down her tank top. There was no way she could make it through offering him coffee. She was mildly hung over, her hair was probably a mess, she had morning breath, and whatever she'd thought she'd seen simply wasn't a thing. He had to go. She needed space to breathe. And think. And breathe. She'd be able to do that once he was gone.

"I should get rolling. I've got a full morning of recording slated." There wasn't a chance in hell she could record with the sandpaper lining her throat, but he didn't need to know that. She headed toward the back door in a clear signal he should leave. He didn't deserve the bum's rush after last night, but embarrassment was stronger than manners.

Caleb slipped on his shoes. "I've got a few things to do myself. But when you break this afternoon, I've got somewhere to take you."

Already off balance, she whipped around and nearly plowed into him. "What? Where? Why?"

Neatly sidestepping, he opened the door himself. "Can't tell you where. I promised Fiona."

"Promised her what, exactly?"

"Can't tell you that either. I have to show you."

She didn't have the brainpower to figure out what the hell her child had talked him into. If she agreed, he'd leave, and then she could shower and get her head on straight. By this afternoon, she'd be back to normal and able to look him in the eye. Then she could figure out whether it was worth trying to ground a college freshman.

"Fine. I should be done around two."

He flashed that easy, familiar smile and her insides went molten. "See you then."

Emerson waited until he'd shut the door and the sound of his footsteps off the deck faded, then she collapsed back against the nearest wall.

What the hell had just happened?

\* \* \*

THE DOG WAS CLEARLY the result of an unholy union between the cat from *Shrek* and a pit bull. It looked up at them from the corner of the kennel with big, liquid eyes that made Caleb want to say, "Take my money!" if only to bring him home and shower him with every dog toy known to man.

The moment Emerson laid eyes on him, she sighed. "Damn it."

Caleb was glad he wasn't the only one.

"I wasn't going to let you talk me into this."

"Fiona thought you'd be lonely without someone to take care of. I wasn't gonna disabuse her of that notion. I just promised to bring you down here to look."

"There's a reason I've never had a dog. They bark. Barking is bad when you make your living recording stuff."

The high-school-aged volunteer piped up, "Actually, I've never heard him bark."

Caleb had noticed that. While practically every other dog in the place was making bids to be noticed, this one hadn't made a peep.

Emerson eyed the boy as if she didn't quite trust him. "Really?"

"He's a funny little dude. Loves to curl up in boxes, like a big cat. The prevailing theory is that he was maybe raised with them."

She hummed a noncommittal note and turned her focus back to the dog.

Caleb couldn't help poking at her, just a little. "Seriously, Em, how can you say no to that face?"

"Plenty of people have," the kid informed them. "He's been here for three months."

"Monsters." Emerson crouched down, curling her fingers through the chain link and making cooing noises.

The dog's little stump of a tail gave a hesitant wag.

"A lot of people are terrified of pit mixes," the volunteer continued.

"Worst smear campaign ever. There's no such thing as bad dogs. Just bad owners," Emerson continued in a sing-song voice.

Caleb and the kid exchanged knowing glances as the dog belly crawled over to sniff her fingers.

"You're just scared and lonely, aren't you, baby? All you want is somebody to love. Isn't that right?"

"We think he's about two. He's heartworm negative, house-trained, and has really good leash manners."

The dog licked her hand, and Emerson scratched his chin in praise. "Can I go in?"

"Sure." The guy opened the kennel for her.

Slowly, Emerson edged inside, moving to the opposite side of the kennel and sitting. She held out a hand and waited, murmuring to the dog in a low voice. Caleb knew from experience how soothing her voice could be. He had a collection of her audiobooks on his phone to listen to on his way to sleep or during downtime at the fire station. The dog was no different. He rose partway to his feet and inched forward, pink-and-black-spotted nose twitching. When he settled his head gently on her knee, Emerson stroked his brown and white ears. The dog let out a sigh, his whole body relaxing.

She swore softly. "Bring me the paperwork."

Two hours later, after an enormously expensive trip to PetSmart, where they'd both been compelled to buy every non-squeaking dog toy on offer, in addition to the essentials, they arrived home with the dog, who still had no name. Emerson took him straight through the house to the backyard, while Caleb hauled in the supplies.

She was leaning against the porch rail, grinning, when Caleb came out to join her. "I think he likes it."

Down below, the dog ran zoomies around the perimeter.

"I'd say so." After last night's tears, he hadn't expected to see that smile so soon. Score one for Fi.

Emerson nudged him in the shoulder, a casual gesture that told him they were back on even footing. "You're really lucky."

Relieved that he hadn't miscalculated by being so bold this morning, he folded his arms on the rail and leaned beside her. "That he's cute? Yeah, I figured that out."

"That, too. But no, that I already have a fenced yard. If I didn't, you'd get drafted to help build me one, since this is all your fault."

"Technically it's Fiona's fault. I was just keeping a promise."

"The pair of you are both sneaky sneaky, and I ought to be mad, but it's hard to hold on to when I see how happy we just made this guy."

The dog had stopped to roll on his back and wriggle on the grass in ecstasy. Emerson laughed. She looked free and unburdened for the first time since he'd known her, and the sight of it struck Caleb in the solar plexus.

"Have dinner with me." The words were out before he could think better of them. Damn it. She'd only just relaxed around him again.

She cut him a glance. "Are you under the impression I can't feed myself if I'm not wrangling a teenager? I promise, I'll eat a vegetable." Amusement glimmered in her eyes instead of this morning's panic. She'd shut him back in that friend box, talking herself out of believing whatever it was that had prompted her to rush him out the door.

Because he didn't want her to forget it, he pivoted toward her, deliberately edging into her personal space to test them both. "You can eat whatever you damn well please. Have dinner with me."

She blinked at him, the smile sliding into confusion as she leaned back, just a little. Caleb liked seeing her off balance, liked knowing he could keep her guessing.

"I appreciate last night. Really, I do. But you don't need to babysit me. I'm not fragile, and I'm not going to fall apart again."

He got that she was embarrassed about last night's breakdown. This, at least, was a worry he could put to rest. "Fragile is the last way I'd ever describe you. You're one of the most terrifyingly competent women I've ever met, and I find that sexy as hell. This is not about babysitting. I want to spend time with you. On a date."

Taking another step toward her, he reached out to cage her against the porch rail, close but not quite touching. He hadn't meant to get into all this quite yet. He'd meant to give her more time. But, after last night...this morning...it was hard to remember why he was still holding back. Hell, hadn't he given her the last four years?

Emerson's mouth dropped open, part surprise, part arousal, if those dilated pupils were any indication. The pulse at the base of her throat fluttered like mad, and a flush worked its way up the column of her lovely throat.

"A date? With me? That's...ridiculous. I'm old enough to be your—"

Caleb arched a brow, waiting for her to finish that sentence. There wasn't *that* big an age gap between them, and what there was had ceased mattering years ago. He was a grown-ass, responsible man attracted to a mature, amazing woman.

"I...I'm older than you."

The stammer almost made him smile. He liked making her nervous. "So?"

A little furrow of consternation dug in between her eyes. He wanted to kiss it away. "So, it's weird."

Yeah, he'd been prepared for this. He knew damned well the only reason they'd gotten this close as friends was because she didn't think he looked at her as a woman. She'd confided, let him in, let him close, without all that self-consciousness because she hadn't been worried about what he thought or trying to impress him. Damn if he didn't love that about her.

"Let's just get clear about this, okay? If we were the same age or I was the older one, would you be hesitating?"

In the face of his logic, she stammered. "I don't—this is weird. We're friends. Neighbors."

He was in it now. Might as well make himself perfectly clear. "And I'd like to be more. If you're legit not interested, that's completely fine. I'll back off right now and we'll go back to the way things were." He hoped like hell she didn't choose door number one. "But if your only hangup about this is some silly number, then I'm sorry to say, I'll have to change your mind."

"Change my—"

Choosing to take that as an invitation—maybe the only one he'd ever get—Caleb captured her mouth with his.

# CHAPTER 5

*A*t the first soft touch of Caleb's lips, Emerson's brain short-circuited, spilling out whatever protest she'd been about to make. Immobile with shock, she could only stand there. No one had kissed her in four years, and never, ever like this.

He wasn't touching her anywhere but her mouth, each tender brush a question that made her knees go weak. That was her only excuse for sagging into him, curling her hands into his shirt. It wasn't because she wanted to get closer for more of this gentle assault on her senses.

But his arms came around her, and one hand slid into her hair, cupping her nape with those strong, capable fingers in a way that made her want to whimper. He angled her head to take the kiss deeper, his tongue tracing the seam of her lips. She opened for him on a greedy moan. But there was no room for embarrassment, only need, as her world tilted again at the taste of him. It hit her blood like a double shot of top-shelf whiskey, lighting her on fire.

Caleb was *kissing* her.

Not a pity kiss. Not a distraction. A toe-curling, no-faking, I-am-into-you kiss. His shorts did nothing to hide his reaction to her. This was not a drill. He was impossibly, improbably into *her*.

And, God, she was so tired of denying her attraction because it had been longer than she could remember since she'd felt like this. Hell, she'd *never* felt like this, and she was so here for this madness.

Sliding her hand up his chest, behind his neck, she dragged him closer. On a groan, he pressed into her, backing her up until she was trapped between his body and the railing. Why wasn't there a wall handy?

His hand slipped beneath her shirt, gliding up her back. Just that simple touch of skin on skin had Emerson rising to her toes and considering climbing him like a tree.

Caleb jolted, his head whipping up. "What the—?"

"Wha—?"

Paws thunked back to the deck. The dog. They'd just been interrupted by the dog. As they watched, he grabbed the hem of Caleb's shorts in his mouth and tugged in a very clear signal to *Get away from my mama.*

The affront on Caleb's face almost made her laugh. Almost. But her lips were still tingling and swollen from the kiss she wished wasn't over. Because now that it was, she could think again.

He let her go and the dog immediately wormed his way between them, plunking his butt down right on Emerson's feet.

Caleb scowled. "Nobody asked you to play chaperone."

It was a good thing he had because they'd been practically dry humping on her back porch. Jesus, had she no self control?

Face flaming, she dropped down to love on her neglected pooch and worked on catching her breath. "You were the one who thought it was a good idea for me to get a dog."

Caleb was still glaring at the canine cock blocker. "We need to have a serious discussion about the roles and responsibilities of a proper wingman." But he softened the words with a rub of the dog's ears. "I'm sure he can be bribed. We'll brainstorm that at dinner."

Dinner. Right. The date.

Without his mouth and hands to circumvent her brain, she was back to remembering all the reasons this was a bad idea. He was younger than her. She was supposed to be working on finding herself again. She was a single parent, and despite his assertion that she was one of the most competent women he knew, she was kind of a mess.

They had chemistry. She could no longer argue that. But was chemistry enough to overcome everything else? To risk one of the best friendships she had?

"Caleb—"

He leaned in and kissed her again, just a quick brush of lips to her temple. "Seriously, Em, age is just a number. Get the anti-wingman here settled, have some bonding time, pick a name. I'll be by to get you tomorrow night at six." And without giving her a chance to respond, he trotted down the steps and out the gate.

Emerson lifted a hand to her lips. She could still feel him, still taste him, and it didn't seem too dramatic to say that nothing would ever be the same again.

Her phone began to ring. Really? Did he think he needed the *last* last word? Rattled and uncertain, she didn't check her phone display before she answered it. "Hello?"

"Oh my God, tell me everything!" Fiona's excited voice nearly pierced her eardrum.

In abject horror, Emerson glanced up at the security camera mounted on the corner of the house. The one pointed in this direction. Holy hell, had Fiona actually *seen* her turn into a mind-less, shameless hussy? Mortification burned through her, molten and bright. She was *not* about to talk about that earth-shattering, mind-bending kiss with her *daughter*. There was only one alternative: Plausible deniability.

"Emerson? Are you there?"

"I...yeah. I'm here, baby. What are you talking about?"

"Don't play coy with me. Caleb texted and said mission accomplished."

"He did *what?*" Her tone was too sharp, but what the hell was he thinking? It was one thing to kiss the bejeezus out of her and scramble her brain. It was something else entirely to tell her kid about it.

"He told me about the dog. Don't be mad. It was my idea, so he was keeping me in the loop."

The dog. She was calling about the dog.

"Oh."

Said dog gazed up at her with undisguised adoration, his whole butt wagging. On a silent breath, she scrubbed his ears and headed inside the house, trying to realign her brain cells to the actual conversation. "I was going to surprise you. I guess you surprised me instead."

"Sooo! Tell me about him!"

This wasn't Paisley. Fi wasn't talking about the details of how Caleb's hard body had felt against hers or how his hand had tangled in her hair as his lips laid absolute waste to her defenses, reminding her in no uncertain terms that she was a woman with long, *long* denied needs.

Digging through the bags he'd piled on the counter, she unearthed a box of dog biscuits and shook it. At the sound, the dog turned joyful circles, his canine grin so wide, it made her laugh. "He's a sweetheart. Two-year-old pittie mix. Dark brown and white, with the cutest little pink and black nose."

"Awwww."

She opened the box. "Want a cookie?"

The dog's trembling butt hit the ground and he looked up with the *Puss In Boots* eyes.

"Oh my God, those eyes. Good boy. Here you go."

He neatly nipped the biscuit from her fingers.

"What's his name?"

As he aimed those deadly eyes at her and lifted a paw, the perfect one came to her. "Mooch. His name is Mooch because I have a feeling that with these eyes, he's gonna be one."

Fiona laughed, and the sound soothed something in Emerson's soul. Her girl was happy. That was what mattered at the end of the day.

"You'll have to send me pictures!"

"I will. You'll have to come meet him. Meanwhile, tell me about school."

"Classes haven't even started yet."

"Humor me. How's the dorm? How's the roommate?"

Deciding she deserved a people cookie after the total upending of her nice, orderly life, Emerson rummaged in the pantry for her emergency stash of Oreos. Package ripped open, she began to munch as Fiona filled her in.

But she couldn't concentrate on the animated descriptions of people living on Fi's floor. Her brain kept drifting back to that kiss and to the dinner date he'd announced. Should she go? She wanted to. And she didn't.

This whole situation absolutely terrified her.

What happened if she indulged in whatever this was and Caleb figured out that she wasn't anywhere near as interesting as he thought? Things would just flame out, and then where would she be? There was no way she could sleep with a man like him and then go back to being *friends*.

But...hadn't he already changed things? Could she really go back to being just buddies after that kiss? Would she ever even be able to *look* at him again without thinking about it?

"—home for dinner tomorrow night?"

"Tomorrow night?" When she was supposed to have a date with Caleb.

She hadn't said yes. He'd just made the declaration. It would serve him right for being dictatorial if Fi was here when he came over. And yet, saying yes to Fiona felt like being a big, fat coward. Wasn't she supposed to be figuring out life without her? Reminding herself of who Emerson Aldridge: Woman actually was? Right now she was still hot and bothered and confused. Surely the best way through that was to go on the date.

"I can't tomorrow, sweetpea. There's something I need to do. How about Tuesday? You can meet Mooch. And I'd love to see you."

"Sounds good. You should invite Caleb."

It was a standard request. Maybe one that should've concerned her before now. They were friends, all of them. Emerson knew she'd crushed on him. That had seemed normal and natural at her age. But...Fiona was in college now. What if she was looking at Caleb as more than a friend? Emerson wasn't at all concerned that Caleb would look back, but what would it do to Fi to find out that the two of them were involved?

Were they involved?

"Emerson?"

"Huh? Oh, sorry. I was just checking the schedule. He's on shift Tuesday night, so it'll be just us girls." And that would be for the best. She didn't want to be around them both at the same time until she'd sorted through how she felt.

"Too bad. But I can't wait to meet Mooch. Give him a kiss for me, and I'll see you Tuesday."

Emerson straightened from the counter and turned. "Sounds like a pl—holy shit!"

"What? Is everything okay?"

"It's fine. I gotta call you back."

She hung up and looked up at the dog, who sat watching her as if she was the greatest thing since bacon. From the top of the refrigerator.

"How the hell did you get up there?"

Mooch grinned.

She lifted her phone and snapped a picture. "Well, life with you definitely isn't going to be boring."

* * *

FRESHLY SHOWERED, Caleb crossed the expanse of yard between his house and Emerson's. He'd had twenty-four hours to wonder whether he'd made a mistake giving her time to think about what had happened between them. But deep down, he knew the full-court press would have backfired on him for sure. Tonight was about addressing whatever concerns she'd come up with—he knew there'd be plenty—and convincing her to give them a chance despite all of them.

Instead of circling around to the back like normal, he went to the front door and rang the bell. She answered a few moments later, a frown bowing her painted lips. She'd done her makeup for him. Nothing outrageous, just some color on her cheeks and lips, and something to make those bluebonnet eyes big enough to drown in. So she did plan on keeping the date. Hurdle number one jumped.

"Why didn't you come to the back?"

"A date seems like a front door kind of event." Caleb stepped inside and brushed a quick kiss to her cheek, catching the subtle floral notes of her shampoo. "You look beautiful."

Her hand fluttered in the air for a moment before tucking a chunk of hair behind her ear. "You didn't say where we were going. I wasn't sure what to wear."

A solid canine head wedged itself between them and began to sniff Caleb from foot to crotch. "Still in chaperone mode, I see." He crouched down on the dog's level to give him a good rubdown instead of letting his gaze linger on the well-worn jeans and form-fitting white cotton shirt that showed off Emerson's curves and a tantalizing hint of skin revealed by the open top buttons.

"You're perfect. I'm grilling at my place so you can bring your new friend here. I figured he might have some separation anxiety this soon." And he knew part of her objections would be tied to what other people would think about her being out with a younger guy. They'd tackle that one later. He wanted her to be comfortable.

As Emerson's whole posture relaxed, he knew he'd made the right call.

"Thanks. I really didn't want to leave him crated. I don't know if he's a digger, and he's got some…unexpected traits that mean I really didn't want to leave him loose in the house on his own." She grabbed the leash and snapped it on. Butt wagging, the dog towed her toward the door.

"Like what? Did he chew up some of your stuff?"

"I'll tell you about it over dinner. Let's just say the theory that he was raised with cats is looking like a good one."

"Curiouser and curiouser."

They crossed the yard together, cutting through his house and out to the patio. Emerson set the dog loose to go sniff the perimeter of his backyard.

"Wine or cider?"

"What's dinner?"

"Got a nice cedar-planked salmon and veggies to toss on the grill."

Her lips curved a little. "Breaking the bachelor mold of steak and potatoes?"

"That's too predictable."

"Nothing about the last few days has been predictable." She blew out a breath. "Surprise me."

He brought back a glass of the sauvignon blanc he knew she liked, along with a plate of stuffed mushrooms. Emerson plucked one off the plate and the dog made a beeline across the yard, plopping down into a vibrating sit.

"Don't even think about it, Mooch. These are not for you."

"You named him Mooch?"

"Seemed appropriate. I mean, look at that face."

Mooch swung The Eyes toward Caleb, determined he didn't have food in his hand, and turned back to Emerson.

"That's Olympic-gold-medal begging right there. Mooch is perfect." He lit the grill. "How's he working out otherwise?"

She sipped her wine, humming in appreciation. "Well, he jumps on counters. And tables. And the refrigerator."

Caleb paused, a mushroom in his hand. "The fridge? How?"

"I don't know. I was on the phone with Fi last night and I turned around and—boom—there he was." She pulled out her phone and swiped the screen. "See?"

Sure enough, the dog smiled down from the top of the fridge. "You can barely even reach that with a stool."

"I am aware. Until I can train him out of it, I've had to move *everything* that's breakable off the horizontal surfaces in the house."

"Yikes. Are you having regrets?" Man, if he'd saddled her with a problem animal...

"No. I mean, there's going to be an adjustment period, but as advertised, he does not, in fact, seem to bark. Like...ever. He stays more or less glued to my side. When I'm recording, he's happy laying down right outside the booth."

"That sounds ideal."

"It's early days yet, but so far, yeah. He's a cuddler. We got him that big, cushy dog bed, and I woke up last night and he'd snuck into my bed, all snuggled up next to me. It was so damned cute, I didn't have the heart to kick him out."

"Well hell, I didn't think I'd be jealous of a dog." The moment the joke left his mouth, Caleb regretted it.

Emerson tensed up again, dropping her gaze to her wine.

"Sorry," he muttered. "I was kidding around. I didn't mean to bring up the elephant in the room."

She shook her head. "We might as well acknowledge it. I don't know what I'm doing here, Caleb. This is crazy."

"You're here because you haven't done anything for yourself since Fiona came into your life." At least, he hoped that was why she was here.

The wine glass made a discordant *thunk* as she set it on the table. "I inherited a traumatized teenager. She needed me, and I—"

Caleb covered her hand with his and squeezed. "No, I'm not saying you should have done any different. I was there that night. I know why you did what you did. It's why I waited."

Confusion drew down her brows. "Waited?"

"I'd have asked you out years ago if you'd had the bandwidth for it. But that wasn't what you needed."

He expected her to fixate on the "years ago" part of his admission, but she surprised him.

"How do you know what I need?" He didn't take offense at the faint edge of accusation in her voice.

"I've made a study of it. A study of you." Because those bluebonnet eyes held a spark of challenge, he began reeling things off. "You need stability and routine. You can pivot when you need to, but it takes a lot out of you. You need physical release for all that stress you carry around like Atlas, which is why I got you into running. You need quiet—until you don't. Not that you've gotten too much of that since Fi came along. Sometimes you need somebody else to pull you out of your shell and your cave. You'll grumble about it a bit, but you almost always end up glad you came." With every word, every statement that showed he'd been paying attention, that he *knew* her, her eyes got rounder, her shock more pronounced. He enjoyed keeping her off balance like this—as long as it meant he was the one who got to catch her.

She was outright staring when he was through. "Why? Why me? I mean, you're—" She waved a hand in his general direction as if to encompass all of him. "—that. You could have any other woman you wanted."

A fact which his fellow firefighters had brought up many times over the years. Not that it mattered.

"I don't want any other woman. I want you." Curling his fingers around hers, he stroked his thumb across her pulse point and felt it jump. "Is that a problem for you? Because I meant what I said. If you don't want to go here, I'm not forcing anything. I'll back off and we'll forget it ever happened."

Her silence stretched out so long, Caleb began to sweat.

"Could you actually forget that kiss?"

Did that mean she could? Or she couldn't?

"Not a chance in hell. I've basically spent every waking minute since I stopped, thinking about doing it again." Might as well embrace the honesty here. "But if that's what you needed me to do, I'd make my best effort."

She looked away, dropping her free hand to Mooch's head and stroking. The dog leaned into her leg in absolute bliss. Lucky bastard.

*Please don't say you want to go back to being friends.* He'd made the promise, and he'd try to keep it, but he didn't know how the hell he'd pull it off. Not now that he knew how she tasted, how well she fit against him, and the sounds she made when—

"I wouldn't have come tonight if I had a problem with it. I just…"

"Just what?"

"I don't understand what you see in me. I mean, you've seen me at my lowest point, my messiest, my least together. What's attractive about that?"

Was she kidding?

"Everything. You've never put on airs, never pretended to be someone you're not. I don't have to wonder if you're going to turn into someone else once the honeymoon period is up because I know you. You're unapologetically you, flaws and all—and I find those pretty charming. That kind of confidence is sexy as hell."

Her laugh was short. "None of that was confidence, Caleb. It was you being out of my age bracket and out of my league besides.

The possibility for anything like this was literally never on my radar."

He didn't like the idea that she thought he was out of her league. It made her sound like she thought she was less than somehow, and that couldn't be further from the truth. But he tackled the part of her statement he actually had an answer for. "Are you still on the age thing? I thought we settled that."

She pursed her lips. "We didn't settle anything. You dictated."

"I did—but only because I knew you'd balk otherwise. But let's circle back because I think this is one of the biggies for you. Why is the age difference an issue? We're both grown adults. We didn't have some prior relationship where you were my babysitter or something. If the situation were reversed and I was the older one, nobody would bat an eye. It always struck me as a weird double standard. What is wrong with two consenting, grown adults of any age being into each other?"

She opened her mouth as if to protest, then closed it again. "You're right. There is no rational reason that an older woman going out with a younger guy is inherently different than the other way around. I can't decide if that makes me feel better or not."

"Why wouldn't it?"

Heat crept into her cheeks. "Because I've felt like such a dirty old woman checking out your ass."

Her admission made him want to do a fist pump and a victory lap around the yard.

"First off, you are nowhere near old or somehow league deficient. Second," he grinned, "you checked out my ass?"

Hiding her face behind her glass, she muttered, "I mean, it's a work of art. It seemed like a crime not to."

"Feel free to have a tactile inspection anytime."

"You're terrible." The blush spread down her throat and into the collar of her shirt. He wondered if it kept going on down to cover those breasts he was trying not to stare at.

"You like it."

She held his gaze for a long, long moment, and Caleb held his breath.

"Yeah, I do."

Lifting her hand, he brushed a kiss to her knuckles. "As far as I'm concerned, that's a good start."

# CHAPTER 6

The broad palm Caleb pressed against her lower back was a distraction as they navigated the crowds of Lower Broadway. She hadn't been up here since the night of the accident—since Blaine. The sight of all the neon signs and honky-tonks had all that old bitterness swirling back up. She'd avoided this place on principle, not wanting to remember that night and everything that came after.

But Caleb had secured tickets to a sold-out show for Kyle Keenan, one of Nashville's up-and-comers. As their first public outing, it was a good choice. No one knew them here. While it wasn't outside the realm of possibility that they could run into someone they knew, it wasn't the same as if they'd gone out in Hamilton. There was a freedom in anonymity. She could focus on them. On him. And he was a helluva thing to focus on.

She still couldn't quite believe Caleb was here with her.

After considerable angsting, she'd made a major effort for tonight, doing up her hair and makeup, pulling out an outfit that showed off attributes she'd forgotten she had. Nothing about her appearance said "mom," and when Caleb periodically looked down at her, his gaze raking over every inch in an appreciative sweep that was almost a physical caress—the only kind she'd gotten since that back deck kiss because he'd slowed way the hell down—it felt *good*. She felt sexy.

He was good at bringing that out in her. Over the past week, he'd managed to convince her he was sincerely into her, and she was no longer certain she was being punked. Mostly, she felt lucky to have snared the interest of a gorgeous, honorable, interesting guy. One who caught the eye of every woman in a thirty-foot radius. It was hard not to preen, just a little, at the looks of envy being shot her way.

Once they reached the venue, Caleb steered her past the entrance, with its trailing line wrapped several layers deep down the sidewalk. Instead, he led her around the corner and down the alley behind the building.

"What are we doing?"

"Going in the back."

"I don't think we can do that."

He flashed those double-barrel dimples and knocked on the door. "You can with my connection."

A tank of a dude, who was obviously a bouncer, opened it. His scowl instantly faded. "Hey, Caleb."

"Hey, Hank."

Hank stepped back and waved them inside. "Come on back."

So Caleb had an in with some of the crew or something? Wow. That was lucky.

They trailed Hank down several narrow corridors before stopping outside a closed door. Hank jerked a head toward it. "He's waiting on you."

"Thanks, man." Caleb saluted him and knocked.

A moment later, the door swung open and Kyle Keenan himself beamed at them. He pulled Caleb into a back-thumping hug. "Been too damned long, man. Come in."

Stunned, Emerson could only follow them inside, cutting a glance at her date. "You know Kyle Keenan?"

Kyle clutched his chest and gave a dramatic stagger. "You wound me, little brother, not telling your lady about me."

"Little brother?" She glanced between the two men, searching Caleb's olive skin and thick, dark hair for any resemblance to the all-American, blue-eyed, blondness of Kyle. If they shared any genetic link, she certainly couldn't see it.

Kyle aimed a Significant Look at Caleb and darted in to catch him in a headlock. They tussled, grunting and laughing in a way that said brothers more clearly than blood ever could.

Caleb twisted out of his grip, holding him at arm's length. "Better not. Be a shame for me to kick your ass right before you go on."

"You wish."

"I'm not scrawny anymore. I lift hoses that weigh more than you every day."

"I still know all the ticklish spots that'll make you say uncle."

Emerson found her lips twitching. "Well, that seems like useful information to have."

Caleb sobered, glaring at Kyle. "Don't even think about it."

"And deprive you of the pleasure of finding them yourself? I would never." Kyle took her hand in a firm shake. His warm smile put her at ease. "Great to finally meet you, Emerson. I've heard a lot about you over the years. Nice to see he finally got up the balls to do something about it."

Scowling, Caleb crossed his arms. "It wasn't about me being a chicken shit."

"Sure it wasn't." Ignoring his brother, Kyle turned back to her. "I understand you're an audiobook narrator?"

"I am."

"I'm a big fan of audiobooks. With my crazy schedule, I don't think I'd ever get a chance to read if I could only do it sitting down. I end up listening while I'm working out or trying to get some downtime on the tour bus."

"They're good for that."

"And you won an Audie a couple years back, right? For one of Dinah McClure's books."

Emerson's jaw dropped. "I...did. How did you know that?" Nobody outside the industry ever seemed to know about the audiobook version of the Emmys.

"Caleb was bust-a-gut proud about it. As he should be. Helluva professional achievement."

She slid him a look, noting a faint hint of color under that dark complexion.

That win was three years ago. He really *had* talked about her a lot, and for a long time, with someone who was some kind of family. It gave credence to his claim of having waited for her for years. She'd glossed over that the other night, but now it circled back around in her brain. He'd truly waited for her to be ready for whatever this was between them. No man had ever paid that much attention, taken that much care with her. But *was* she ready?

Somebody knocked on the dressing room door. "Fifteen minutes."

"That's my cue." Kyle flashed another broad smile. "Emerson, great to meet you."

"And you. My daughter's never going to believe I met you."

"Fiona, right? Caleb mentioned she'd just headed off to college." If Kyle thought it was weird that she had a college-aged kid, he didn't show it.

"She has."

"Let's torture her a little. Take a pic of us, little bro." He wrapped a loose arm around her shoulders and they both mugged for the camera.

"Best wait to send that until after the show," Emerson warned. "Otherwise she's going to be blowing up both our phones."

"Fair point." Caleb turned to his brother. "Are you in town for a bit?"

"Yes, thank Jesus. I've had about enough of the road and Mercy Lee's bullshit. Let's get dinner and catch up before I head back out

58

on the road again. Emerson, I hope you'll come. I'd love to get to know you better."

Caleb's brother or not, having dinner with a country music singer with no little bit of name recognition firmly put her life in the category of surreal. "That would be…great."

"Have a good show tonight, bro. Text me. We'll figure out time and place."

Then they were being led down more labyrinthine halls and to their seats.

Once they were settled at one of the small, high-top tables right near the stage, she propped her chin in one hand. "Well, you're full of surprises. Why didn't you ever mention you were related to Kyle Keenan?"

Those big shoulders bunched in a shrug. "It's complicated. And he's not somebody famous to me. He's just Kyle. But I thought you might enjoy coming out."

She wondered about those complications. As well as she knew him, there were significant gaps in his past she wasn't familiar with. But now wasn't the time to ask. "I really am. I haven't been down here in years." She looked around, taking in the intimate space, already packed with other patrons.

"Why is that? Not a fan of crowds?"

"Not especially. Super crowded venues mean lots of noise, and I can't really talk easily under those conditions and still protect my voice. But I do enjoy good music, so I don't mind putting up with them for that."

He studied her, those dark eyes always seeming to see too much. "I feel like there's more to the story."

Might as well put it out there so he knew where she was coming from. "The last time I came down here, I was out with Paisley and her guy of the month." She told him about the karaoke bar and finding Blaine with his tongue down the blonde's throat.

"Asshole." Though his tone was mild, Caleb's eyes were hot

with temper. "Is that why I've never seen you out with anybody in all these years?"

"Partly. It was also the night of the accident. I'd just left there when you called me. So then there was Fiona. After that, it just didn't seem worth it to try. I didn't have the emotional bandwidth to cope with the disappointment on top of everything she needed."

Which Caleb had understood. She was only just starting to fully grasp what he'd done for her and wonder about the depth of feeling that lay under that decision. Nobody waited four years, put in all that effort toward friendship, for someone who was only a passing crush. That scared the hell out of her. What were his expectations? Could she possibly meet them?

She wanted to. She wanted to deserve all that attention and effort. A part of her wanted to drop all her guards, all that caution, and throw herself into this full-force. But she wasn't at all sure she could trust her own judgment in this arena.

The crowd began to cheer, drawing their attention to the stage, where Kyle and his band were filing out and taking their positions for this unplugged show. Caleb scooted his barstool next to hers, draping an arm along the back.

"Good evening, Nashville!" Kyle called.

The audience whooped and hollered.

"It's been a minute since I've been back in this neck of the woods, and it's always nice to be on home turf. I wanna give a special shout out to my brother and his girl, who came out tonight."

Caleb's girl. The words shot a surprising thrill through her.

She might not know a hundred percent how she felt, but she knew she appreciated this man and all his thoughtful consideration. So she leaned into his side, brushing a kiss to the underside of his jaw before settling into his embrace to enjoy the show.

* * *

"HOW THE HELL did he get up there?" Roadie asked.

Caleb squinted at the picture Emerson had texted of herself pointing over her shoulder at Mooch, who lay stretched out on top of the upper kitchen cabinets. Her face asked the same question. "Apparently nobody ever told him he wasn't a cat."

"Damnedest thing I ever saw."

Caleb couldn't stop the dopey grin as he texted back. **Does he need a rescue?**

He'd take any excuse to pop over and see her.

He didn't usually mind his two days on, three days off schedule. He enjoyed most of the work, whether he was fighting fires, out on medical calls, or just hanging around the firehouse shooting the shit while cleaning equipment and running drills. But that had been before he'd started dating Emerson. Now he was counting the hours until his shift was over, like they hadn't been spending every non-work hour together the past three weeks. But damn, after waiting all this time, he didn't want to waste a minute.

"Awww, lookit, y'all! Grad's texting his *girlfriend*," Pork Chop cooed.

Without even looking, Caleb shot up his middle finger. "You just wish you had a woman half as amazing as Emerson."

Fonzie flipped a chair around and straddled it. "You sure she's not just trying you on for size like a fancy pair of shoes?"

"Did you seriously just compare me to a pair of shoes?"

"I'm just sayin'. Lot of those single moms like to do that while they're figuring out their shit. Try a guy out as a fun little novelty. Especially the pretty ones. Doesn't mean they're gonna keep you at the end of the day."

"If she doesn't keep you, it means you weren't treating her right to begin with." Caleb had the lock on that. He'd had years to plan how to woo this woman.

"I don't know about novelty, but I wouldn't get too comfortable. Single moms are always gonna put the kids first. That's a fact," Showboat announced.

"Fiona's in college, and a great kid to boot."

"And yeah, that's great. Package deal, you better like the whole package for sure. But you gotta be prepared to always come second. I'm not. It's why I don't date single moms."

Caleb crossed his ankles and stretched out in his chair. "I don't have the same titanic ego you do. I don't need to be the center of the universe."

The guys roared with laughter and laid into Showboat as the fresh target of ribbing.

"In all seriousness, we just wanna make sure Grad watches himself," Klunker weighed in. "He's been building this up all this time. It can't possibly be as smooth sailing as he's imagining."

Rolling his eyes, Caleb shoved up out of his chair and put the med kit away. "You all have a very dim view of relationships with complicated women."

"Women aren't supposed to be complicated," Fonzie declared.

Peach, the lone woman in the company, clocked him in the face with a pair of rolled up socks. "And we see why you're still single."

Cue Ball, their captain, waded into the laughter. "Ignore them. Single moms are people worthy of love, same as everyone else. Just take it slow and don't get in over your head or get ahead of yourself." As he had himself married a single mom of two ten years ago, Caleb figured he was the only one of the bunch with anything worth listening to.

"Hey Grad, you've got a visitor." Roadie stepped aside to reveal Emerson, a massive plastic container in her hands and a hesitant smile on her face.

Caleb shot out of his chair. "Hey! What are you doing here?"

"I come bearing cookies. Oatmeal chocolate chip."

The stupid grin popped out again. She'd made his favorite cookies.

"They seemed like a good excuse to stop by to see you."

Caleb took her hand, reeling her in. "You don't need an excuse."

"I can just...relieve you of those so you have your hands free." Peach gently extricated the box from her grip.

"If y'all wipe out my cookies before I get any, I will cheerfully murder you all," Caleb announced, then pulled Emerson in for the kiss he really wanted.

He swallowed her little squeak of surprise, relishing her surrender by degrees, until she stopped noticing the adolescent *ooooing* happening around them and gave herself over to the kiss. To him. Yeah, he needed this. Needed the taste of her and that quiet sound of pleasure in her throat. He needed everything from this woman.

"Oh my God," Roadie moaned, his mouth full. "You need to marry her. Marry her right now so she can supply us with cookies for life."

Caleb lifted his head and spied everybody with cookies in their hands. "Hey! Paws off my cookies."

"Oh, come on, Grad, you got something sweeter right there," Cue Ball said.

Emerson tucked into his side. "Grad?"

"You know like *The Gr—*" Fonzie's words cut off at the quick elbow from Peach, but not before realization dawned.

"Like *The Graduate*," Emerson finished. An embarrassed flush worked its way up her throat. "Jesus, I'm not *that* much older than him."

"No, you're not. Ignore them. They're ridiculous." Caleb pivoted to put himself between Emerson and his crew, wanting to shield her from their teasing. It was one thing for him to be a target. Ribbing was part of the teambuilding experience. But she was another thing entirely. She'd only barely managed to get over her own issues with the age gap.

"If it makes you feel any better, he was Torch for years before that," Klunker offered.

"Because he carried one for you," Pork Chop clarified.

Now it was Caleb's turn to feel the creep of heat in his cheeks. He wasn't embarrassed about his feelings for Emerson. He'd been honest about how long he'd had them. But he didn't think she'd really believed him.

Her lips twitched as she gave him a speculative look.

"Do I even want to know what's going through that brain of yours right now?"

"I was just wondering if that made you my own personal Johnny Storm."

As the rest of his company whooped with laugher, he grinned. "Flame on, baby."

Was he imagining that spark of heat in her eyes? The curl of her fingers at his waist said no. His pulse leapt. Since that first, out-of-this-world kiss, he'd slowed things way down, letting her set the pace. Going from friends to more was a big change for her, and he didn't want to rush her. But, God, he ached with wanting her.

With one last squeeze, she stepped back. "I need to get going. I know you're busy, and I need to drive on into Nashville to take Fiona her cookies. Oatmeal chocolate chip are her favorites."

Fiona's favorites.

It didn't mean anything. Oatmeal chocolate chip cookies were awesome. They were lots of people's favorites. And of course, if Emerson had gone to the trouble to make cookies, she was going to make enough for Fi. She'd thought of him. And she'd made the effort and come here first. Because she wanted to see him.

*What the hell is wrong with you? It's not a contest.*

He'd let his idiot coworkers get to him.

"Tell her hi for me."

"Will do. Although you're still on her shit list for not getting *her* tickets to see Kyle Keenan."

Caleb snorted. "Can't have that. I'll get her an autograph."

"She'd love that. Now go rescue your cookies while there are still some left. I'll see you when you get off?"

"Absolutely."

He'd be counting the minutes.

# CHAPTER 7

"*I* don't know what's gotten into you, but this latest book is absolutely amazeballs," Paisley gushed. "I mean, it's not like your normal work is shoddy by any stretch, but this one is just next level."

Emerson had to admit, to herself at least, that she was right. "Glad you're happy with it. I'll get those corrections done tomorrow, and Troy should have the final audio files ready for you by the end of the week."

"Fabulous. My readers are going to go nuts. I swear, if I didn't know any better, I'd say you've suddenly started having really great sex."

She bit her lip as her brain readily supplied a mental image of Caleb in turnout pants...and nothing else, doing a slow striptease.

Paisley didn't miss a thing. "*Emerson! Are you?*"

"I'm not. But...I'm thinking about it."

At her friend's squeal, Mooch abandoned his impression of a throw rug and began to dance in place, certain a cookie was imminent.

"With *who?*"

She almost hated to admit it because she knew the explosion of squee that was coming.

"Caleb."

"Oh my God! Tell me everything. What are you planning? Slow seduction? I'm a fan of just planting a big one on them. Saves confusion."

Digging a dog biscuit out of the tin from the pantry, Emerson took Mooch through his paces of sit-shake-lay down. "Actually, he planted a big one on me."

"I *knew* it! I *knew* he was into you." Paisley did a victory boogie that sent Mooch into another fit of spins. "When?"

"A few weeks ago."

"A few *weeks*? And I'm only just now hearing about it? That is a violation of the Best Friend Code! Why didn't you tell me?"

"I felt...weird. And I wasn't sure what I was going to do about it."

"Do about it? Girl, you jump that. That's what you do about it."

"It's not that simple. He's one of my best friends. I don't want to take the idea of changing that lightly."

Paisley reined in her enthusiasm. "Okay, okay. I've written enough friends-to-lovers romances to understand that. How did it happen? Was it one of those situational deals where the sexual chemistry just exploded into a kiss that surprised you both?"

"I think I was the only one surprised. Apparently, he's been wanting to date me for a while."

"How long is a while?"

She bit her lip. "Um...years."

Clutching her chest, Paisley feigned a swoon. "Years?"

Emerson explained why he'd waited and what she'd found out about his nicknames at the firehouse the other day.

"That is so romantic. It's official. This man is a unicorn, and you need to marry him and have his babies."

She narrowed her eyes. "I literally just got the first one out of the house."

"Fine. Skip the babies. But please bang his brains out. You're at your sexual peak. So is he. May you make beautiful orgasms together. Many, many orgasms to make up for your long dry spell."

Emerson swallowed a snicker. "I appreciate your enthusiasm. I am, as I said, considering it. We're taking things slow. I wouldn't hop into bed with any guy after only dating a few weeks. Not that there's anything wrong with that. It's just not how I'm wired."

"Yeah but it's not like you're starting from scratch here. You've known him for years. You *know* him. What's stopping you from mapping the Abs of Glory with your tongue?"

*That* mental image had Emerson's cheeks heating, even as she dropped her gaze. "I just...I guess I keep waiting for him to change his mind."

"About what?"

"About me. What the hell is he doing with me when he could have basically any woman out there with a tighter, younger body and none of the baggage?"

When Paisley said nothing, Emerson dared a glance up.

Her friend's scowl was ferocious. "There is so much wrong with what just came out of your mouth, I don't even know where to start. First off, every-damn-body has baggage. That's life. And Caleb is perfectly well aware of yours. He's still here. Second, have you looked in a mirror? You're gorgeous. All that running has done amazing things for your legs and ass, and I hate you a little bit for it, but not enough to start running myself. Third...you two are *friends*. You are not a surprise to him, and he is clearly into you, exactly as you are. Do you have any idea what a gift that is? Fourth, he is not Blaine. He's been waiting for you for four years. No way in hell is he going to go off searching for greener pastures."

"But what if...what if I disappoint him in bed? It's been a *really* long time, and I—"

"Oh, shut up. You are certified, grade-A, whatever the top of the line thing is in organic grass for him. And it will be great between you because you've got that foundational emotional connection. So stop acting like you're old because you *inherited* a kid who is now eighteen and go jump the man. You know you want to."

She really, really did.

The knock on the back door had Mooch abandoning his pursuit of cookie to go streaking across the kitchen. A moment later, Caleb stepped in. Everything in Emerson simultaneously relaxed and sped up at the sight of him crouching down to love on her dog—the toll Mooch dictated must be paid to get to her.

If he saw Paisley, he gave no indication. His eyes stayed fixed on her as he discharged his canine adoration duty and crossed over. He was still dressed in the HFD t-shirt and navy cargo pants that were his uniform, his hair obviously wet from a shower.

"Hey, you."

Because the low rumble of his voice stoked the desire that had been at a steady simmer for days, Emerson rose up to her toes to kiss him. The proverbial cat was out of the bag now, so why the hell not?

He pulled her tight against his chest—Abs of Glory indeed—and his mouth took a lazy tour of hers. She could get drunk on the taste of him. That seemed like a magnificent way to spend an hour or thirty. Exploring every toned inch of him with her tongue and teeth and—

As heat pooled between her thighs, she considered maybe there *was* something to this whole sexual peak thing.

Caleb eased back, leaving her breathless. "Missed you."

And those simple words turned her heart to marshmallow fluff. Not "missed this." Missed her. He cared about *her*. Had talked enough about her that *both* of his nicknames at the firehouse stemmed from his interest. She was over here freaking out that he was going to change his mind about her and everywhere she looked was evidence of his constancy. That was next-level romance. What the hell was she waiting for?

She stroked her fingers over the fine hair at his nape. "Missed you back."

Those double-barreled dimples popped.

"Hey, Paisley."

"Hey, Caleb."

At the syrupy sweet tone, Emerson looked over to find her sporting a Cheshire Cat grin and a giant two thumbs up.

"I take it you approve?" he asked.

"Oh, you have no idea." She walked over to snatch her purse. "I should get out of your way."

"Don't leave on my account."

Paisley met Emerson's gaze and executed some kind of exaggerated morse code with her eyes that was about as subtle as a Panzer tank. "No, no. I just stopped by to talk to Em about my audio proofs. I look forward to those final files."

"Are these the ones for *There You'll Be?* Because I really need to know how you're going to sort things with Sarah and Rhett. You dropped a really hard stinger for that in the last book, and I just don't see how he's going to redeem himself."

They both stared at him, dumbfounded.

He blinked. "What?"

Emerson found her voice first. "You…read romance?"

"I've read all the books you've narrated."

"All of them?" she squeaked. That was…hundreds.

Caleb shrugged without an ounce of self-consciousness. "I love your voice. I got a bunch of the guys at the station on them, too. If they weren't too embarrassed to admit it, they'd thank you for upping their game with the ladies."

He was custom-made, walking foreplay. This man really was a unicorn. It was time she stopped denying that.

"Paisley."

"Yup. Going. Talk to you tomorrow. Or, you know, next week. Whenever."

"Let the dog out back, will you?"

"Sure thing. Byyyyyyye!"

The door shut behind her and Mooch.

Caleb went brows up. "Well that was a quick departure. What was that about?"

"This."

Fisting her hands in his shirt, she dragged his mouth to hers.

CALEB HAD SPENT considerable time thinking about how to seduce this woman. He'd imagined taking his time, unwrapping her literal and metaphorical layers and steeping her in pleasure, until she forgot anyone who'd come before him. But something had flipped a switch in her. The moment Emerson's lips touched his, he understood that whatever deceleration he'd initiated was over. She was zero to ninety in less than a second, her mouth taking his in a devouring kiss that bordered on savage.

*Thank Christ.*

The needs he'd ruthlessly leashed for years strained against his control, begging to meet that desperation head-on. But no matter what she wanted, he wasn't settling for hard and fast. Not this first time.

Sliding a hand into her hair, he angled her head, taking control of the kiss and diving deep. Her moan of pleasure as his tongue stroked against hers had his blood leaping from simmer to boil. Hands streaking up his chest, she locked her arms around his neck, rising up to wrap one leg around his hips, lining up her center with his straining erection. As she began to rock, taking the pleasure she wanted, he felt his grip on control slipping. Needing more, he boosted her up and backed her against the nearest wall, grinding against her.

Emerson's head fell back on a groan. "Caleb." His name on her lips was both prayer and plea. "I need you inside me."

Growling, he tightened his hold, every cell wanting to claim her right here, right now. But damn it, this was Emerson. He'd been waiting so damned long for her. He wasn't about to take her against the wall like some kind of mindless animal. All but drunk with desire, he turned and moved toward the hall. Her tongue traced the shell of his ear, and his knees wobbled. He could get them up the stairs to a bed without injury. Probably.

She bit gently at the lobe. "Too far. Sofa."

By some divine intervention, he made it to the couch, turning at the last moment, so it was him who crashed down, taking the brunt of the impact. Emerson wasted no time, straddling his lap so his hard-on was nestled in the softness between her thighs. Purring at the contact, she arched back, stripping her shirt up and off.

Caleb thanked the gods of lingerie for this confection of peach satin and lace offering up her breasts like a gift. "Fuck, you're beautiful."

"Your turn."

At her rasped order, he dragged his t-shirt off with one hand and tossed it to the floor. Then he reached for her, skimming his palms up the silk of her skin to cup her breasts, testing the weight of them in his palms. Her breath went short, her nipples pearling against the fabric as he stroked his thumbs over them. He wanted her bare for him, wanted her writhing. Beneath him. Over him. He just plain wanted her.

"Do you have any idea how long I've dreamed about tasting you?"

She reached back and released the clasp. The bra fell away, spilling those glorious breasts into his hands. Her eyes glimmered like blue flame. "There's nothing stopping you."

Needing no further permission, Caleb pulled one rosy nipple into his mouth. As he circled it with his tongue, she swiveled her hips, rocking against his erection. Every gasp and moan spurred him on. She was a fever in his arms, so responsive to every touch and taste. Hands braced on his shoulders, she bowed back, pressing more firmly into his mouth, his hands, as her hair spilled down her back and she rode him. He didn't know what he'd expected, but her complete lack of inhibition as she chased her pleasure wasn't it, and that was pretty much the hottest thing he'd ever seen. Watching her face as he drove her higher had his balls tightening, but he held back, focused on getting her up and over that first peak, licking and sucking until she shot over on a scream that damned near had him coming in his pants like a teenage boy.

Before she'd even begun to come down from the high, her hands were fumbling between them for his belt. "Need you inside me. Now."

Caleb gripped her hips, starting to shift her off his lap to remove her shorts. From the coffee table the laptop began to ring. Emerson jerked in shock and toppled backward before he could catch her.

"Shit! Are you okay?"

But she wasn't even looking at him as she scrambled up from the floor. "Oh my God, Fiona." Grabbing up a shirt, she dragged it on. "I have to take this."

Was she serious?

As she turned the laptop away and plopped herself in a chair, he realized she was.

"Just...stay over there. Okay?"

Caleb glanced down at his crotch, where his dick hadn't gotten the message that their impulsive plans had been derailed. Yeah, no, he wasn't hopping on this call with that flag still flying. Sinking back onto the sofa, he scrubbed both hands over his face and wondered if Emerson would make it quick so they could pick back up where they left off.

"Hey baby. How's everything going?"

"It's going. Sorry for the unplanned video call, but I tried your phone and you didn't answer and I know you were probably in the booth but I thought—Is that Caleb's shirt?"

He looked over in time to see Emerson freeze. Sure enough, it was his T-shirt she'd grabbed off the floor. She glanced down at the HFD logo, her brain obviously whirring. Caleb knew she hadn't told Fiona about them yet. As close to the vest as she was playing it, revealing their involvement while wearing his shirt and with almost-sex hair was definitely not at the top of her list for ways to announce it.

"What? Oh, no. I picked it up at one of their fundraisers a while back."

Like Fi didn't realize the HFD never sold their shirts as part of a fundraiser?

"Huh. I don't remember seeing it before."

"It was pre-you. I'm behind on laundry, so I'm digging deep into the t-shirt drawer."

He was pretty sure Fiona wasn't buying any of this, but she didn't call Emerson on it, and he figured letting his woman have her delusion was the quickest path to getting back to the naked portion of the evening.

"So, I need your help."

Emerson straightened, Mom-mode clearly engaged. "With what?"

"I kinda left my headlights on and accidentally locked my keys in the car. Can you bring the spare set?"

Caleb looked at his crotch. *Sorry, pal.*

"Where are you?"

Fiona listed a location that had him straightening. Not a great part of town. What the hell was she doing down there? He started to move toward the chair to ask himself, but Emerson waved for him to stay out of the frame.

"Are you by yourself?"

"Yeah. I'm sorry. I should have paid more attention."

"It happens to the best of us. Drop me a pin with your location. I'm on my way."

"Love you, Auntie Em."

"Love you, too. See you in a bit."

She ended the call and winced. "It seems we're going to have to take a raincheck on naked time. Duty calls."

"I get it. She comes first." That was as it should be, no matter how much he was hating the teenager interruptus at the moment. He tugged Emerson out of the chair, sliding his hands beneath the shirt to stroke over the smooth skin of her back. "I'll come with you."

She shook her head. "No way. If I show up with you, she's going to cop to what we were up to when she called."

Disappointment pinched at her reluctance. He was proud to be with her and wanted to shout it from the rooftops. "You have to tell her about us sometime."

"I know. I'm sorry. I just...not like that." She framed his face in her palms. "I don't want to just spring it on her. Because it's you. Because you're friends, and I don't want to make things weird between you."

Caleb could hear the *if we don't work out and things get weird between us* that she didn't say.

*One step forward, two steps back.*

He thought of Cue Ball's advice. *Don't get ahead of yourself.*

For all that being with Emerson felt easy for him, it was still new for her. She needed time to settle into this dynamic. She wasn't hiding him like some dirty secret, and it was her prerogative to tell Fiona however she thought best, no matter how much it might chafe his own desires. She'd get there in her own time. He just had to be patient.

"Fair enough." He pulled her closer, not wanting to let her go just yet. "I could stick around, hang with Mooch until you get back. Invent new ways to pick up where we left off."

She stretched up on her toes, pressing her breasts against his chest. "As appealing as that sounds, I'm probably going to have to take her to get a new battery—this one's been on the edge for a while—and I've got an early day of recording tomorrow. I really can't afford to have you keep me up screaming all night."

The list of ways he could do that began scrolling through his head, draining all his blood south again. "I didn't imagine you were a screamer."

"I never have been before." Her cheeks colored at the admission.

And he hadn't even gotten her fully naked yet. "For the record, I really fucking loved it."

"Me too." She brushed a quick kiss over his lips. "I know it's not necessarily romantic, but maybe it's better if we plan for this. I can clear my schedule for the next day and you can have your wicked way with me so if I lose my voice it's not a problem."

The idea of worshiping every inch of her until she'd screamed herself hoarse made him feel like a god. He dropped his hands to her ass and pulled her against the erection that was stirring to fresh life at the prospect. "Challenge accepted at the earliest opportunity."

"Can't wait."

Neither could he.

# CHAPTER 8

*E*merson should never have made an actual *plan* to sleep with Caleb. Rookie mistake. The Universe had taken it as a dare and continually thrown a monkey wrench into the works at every opportunity. She'd had last-minute work dropped on her by a high-profile client she didn't dare refuse. Caleb had been pulled in to cover two extra shifts in the last ten days. They'd managed to steal an hour here or there, but any time they rounded to third base, it was like a warning bell sounded and a new interruption showed up. She was going crazy with want and wondered what atrocity she'd committed in a past life that merited this level of punishment.

Tonight they had plans for dinner with Kyle before he left town to resume his tour with Mercy Lee Bradshaw. And after... after their social duties were discharged, she was finally taking Caleb to bed. With that in mind, she'd scrubbed, buffed, shaved, and moisturized, capping the whole thing off with a sexy set of lingerie beneath her dress. All the prep had been worth it for the look on his face when he came to pick her up. Big Bad Wolf personified.

Every inch of her skin felt electrified, every atom pulling

toward him. Now that the touch barrier had been broken, it seemed they both craved that connection. He kept his palm on her thigh the whole drive, and she found herself eying side streets, wondering if they could find an out-of-the-way spot to christen his truck like a couple of horny teenagers. How in the hell was she supposed to focus on being polite and social and interesting when all she could think about was getting Caleb naked and having those calloused hands on every inch of her body?

At the restaurant, he checked his phone. "Looks like Kyle's running a little late. You want to wait out here or go inside?"

"Better go inside. If you keep looking at me like that, I'm going to give in to the urge to steam up the windows, public decency be damned."

The low rumble of his chuckle shot straight to her core. "Fair enough. You look good enough to eat tonight."

"God, I hope so."

After a beat of silence, he threw back his head and laughed full out. "Oh, I really like this side of you." He slid out of the truck and came around to open her door, leaning in to murmur in her ear as he helped her down. "And, for the record, I absolutely intend to have you for dessert."

Emerson squeezed her thighs together. So this was how the night was going to go. Blatantly suggestive flirting to torture each other until they could finally, *finally* act on it. The anticipation might kill her.

Caleb offered his arm. "Milady."

She took it, relishing the possessive feel of having her hands on him in public. Whatever qualms she'd had about being seen out with a younger guy had been burned away—likely by frustrated lust. So her head was high as they strode into the restaurant.

Caleb put his name on the waitlist with the hostess and turned to her. "You want to wait at the bar?"

Before she could answer, someone called out. "Emerson Aldridge, is that you?"

She turned to see Peggy Barclay, one of the moms she'd served with on the high school theater fundraiser committee. Peggy had a daughter Fiona's age, though she hadn't been part of Fi's friend group.

"Why, I didn't recognize you." The sugary-sweet tone of this pronouncement was accompanied by a head-to-toe inventory of Emerson's appearance that clearly found her to be inappropriate. The thigh-skimming dress and knee-high boots were sexier than anything she'd worn during her stint working bake sale booths or ticket sales, but it hardly merited the streetwalker judgment in the other woman's eyes.

Determined to be polite, Emerson forced a smile. "Peggy, hi."

Caleb's arm slipped around her waist, and she instantly relaxed.

The other woman's eyes widened slightly before she caught herself. "How is Fiona?"

"All settled in at school. What about Erin? She's at University of Alabama, isn't she?"

They chatted for a few minutes about the girls, with Peggy's gaze slipping repeatedly to Caleb, clearly waiting for an introduction. Emerson was having way too much fun letting her stew and wonder who he was.

At last, the older woman couldn't take it anymore. "Are you going to introduce me to your...friend?"

Caleb, who'd patiently waited through the exchange, offered his free hand. "Caleb Romero. Emerson's boyfriend."

They hadn't had that discussion defining what they were, but she found she loved being publicly claimed by him.

Peggy seemed momentarily stunned. "Aren't you Mr. January?"

*Huh.* The older woman hadn't struck Emerson as the type to indulge in something like a sexy firefighter calendar.

"Sure am." He winked and flashed her the double dimples.

There was another back-and-forth glance between them, as if Peggy couldn't work out how the hell they made any sense.

Emerson had mostly found her Zen about that particular topic. Were they unconventional as a couple? Sure. Did she give a damn about that anymore? Not even a little bit.

An older man with silver-shot brown hair joined Peggy. "The table's nearly ready, hon."

"Ed, you remember Emerson Aldridge. Fiona's mother."

"Of course. Good to see you again, Emerson." There wasn't a trace of his wife's vitriol in the tone or affable expression.

"And this is Caleb Romero. Her boyfriend." The faint emphasis on the last word seemed to highlight her incredulity.

Ed brightened as he offered his hand to Caleb. "You work with our son, Davis, I believe."

Caleb's smile shifted to a more natural one. "You're Pork Chop's parents? Nice to meet you. Your son is turning out to be a fine firefighter."

He worked with one of Peggy's children? That was...weird. Wasn't it? She was trying to remember how many of them there were when Kyle stepped up to the group.

"Hey, y'all. Sorry I'm late."

Emerson almost laughed at the Clark Kent glasses he wore, but it seemed to do the trick. No one around them gave him more than a passing glance, not even Peggy and Ed, who looked right at him as he offered a polite nod.

The hostess called Caleb's name.

"Excuse us. That's our table." He steered Emerson away.

She was still chewing over the interaction by the time they were settled into a booth and had given their drink orders.

"Okay, what's bugging you?" Caleb prodded.

"You work with her son?"

"Sure. He's one of our probies. Came on last year after getting out of the academy. Good kid."

"How old is he?"

Caleb blew out a breath. "Are we on this again?"

"Just...how old?"

"I don't know. Twenty? Twenty-one, I think. It doesn't mean anything."

"No, but it does." At the frustration building on his face, she lifted her hands for peace. "Roll with me for a minute. I'm having an epiphany. I spent the last four years working with that woman on committees at the high school. I never *once* thought about how old she is. I don't think she ever realized how old I was either. Our kids were the same age and that was the end of it."

Caleb and Kyle were staring at her like she was a little off her rocker. Maybe she was. How had this never occurred to her before?

"Peggy's got two college-aged kids and her husband is in his mid-fifties, easy. I've got a college-aged kid and you, Mr. Young, Hot, and Studly."

Kyle snickered.

"Yeah..." Caleb drew the word out, clearly not understanding the significance.

"I never told her Micah and I were in high school when Fiona was born. Why would I? It wasn't their business, and I saw the judgement Micah got over the years as other parents did the math to figure out she was a teenage mother. When I inherited Fiona, nobody questioned it. They didn't know Micah, didn't know the history. I was just there, and they made assumptions about me. Most of the parents of kids her age are probably a good decade older than me."

"Is that a surprise?" Kyle asked, as the waitress set their drinks on the table.

"Honestly, yes. I came to this whole parenting thing late in the game, straight into the deep end. There was so much stress and worry, it's like I aged five years mentally for every year that passed since the accident. This is the first time in forever that I don't feel *old*. I feel like...me again." She laughed, feeling a weight slide off her shoulders. "I am not a cougar for dating you."

Caleb's brows drew together. "Haven't I been saying that for a month?"

Emerson wrapped her arm around his and leaned close. "Yes. But the difference is, now I believe it."

His dark eyes kindled as he covered her hand with his. "Then I'd say that's something to celebrate."

She lifted her wine. "I'll drink to that."

\* \* \*

CALEB PULLED his brother in for a back-thumping hug. "Call me when you get back in town."

"Will do. Pray I don't get arrested for diva-cide on this last leg of the tour."

"Is Mercy Lee really that bad?" Emerson asked.

"You know those reality TV shows about pageant moms? Picture that kind of crazy, but younger and hotter, with the voice of a country angel."

Her mouth quirked into an amused smile as she slid an arm around Caleb's waist, snuggling into his side. "Have you and she ever…?"

"Oh, hell no. I don't want any part of that shit."

Caleb tugged her closer. "Kyle likes his women sane, willing to call him on his shit, and unimpressed with his fame. Or he did, once upon a time."

The good humor his brother had sported all night faded. "You and I both know I fucked that up but good."

"Apologies fix a lot of shit." And as far as Caleb knew, he'd never even tried in all these years.

Kyle shook his head. "Not this."

For a moment, regret flickered over his face, and Caleb wondered what would happen if somebody locked him and Abbey in a room. Would they finally talk about it? Or would they both continue to stubbornly cling to old hurts?

Tapping the hood, Kyle circled around to the driver's side of his car. "I gotta go. You two crazy kids have fun. Emerson, great to see you again."

Caleb shook his head as Kyle shut the door and started the engine. "Stubborn bastard."

"What was all that about?"

"Him being a dumbass. But that's not my story to tell." Not interested in wasting any more time contemplating his brother's failed love life, he looked down at her. "You ready to head home?"

Her pupils sprang wide, bottomless pools he wanted to drown in. "So ready."

Caleb's heart tripped into a gallop. *Finally.*

They both knew what was coming, and he couldn't fucking wait. Tension and awareness crackled around them as they slid into the truck.

She blew out a breath, dropping her head back against the seat. "I'm about ready to explode from anticipation." Rolling her head, she caught his gaze. "I want your hands on me, Caleb."

More than willing to accommodate her, he laid a palm on the warm, satiny skin of her thigh, inching it higher. One of them could get started on this party already.

But Emerson stopped him with a low laugh. "Much as I would likely enjoy that, I want your focus on the road instead of my hair-trigger orgasm."

He loved that hair-trigger orgasm, loved knowing he could bring her to the edge so quickly. But she had a valid point. Driving called for the big boy brain, and he was already down a significant amount of blood-flow. "Fair enough." But he kept his hand on her as he navigated the streets of Hamilton, back to Pin Oak Drive.

As soon as he pulled into his garage, Caleb threw the truck into park, unfastened her seatbelt and dragged her into his lap so she straddled him. Her dress rode up, displaying a tantalizing hint of silk between her thighs. He nudged the hem higher to get a better look and saw the panel was already soaked through.

Drawing one finger slowly up her center, he fixed his eyes on hers. "As soon as we make it inside, I'm peeling these right off you and making myself at home between these gorgeous legs. I want to taste what I do to you."

She whimpered, her eyes dropping to half mast. "Caleb."

"I want to feel you come all over my tongue and my fingers and my cock—preferably in that order—before we start all over again."

"You have no idea how on board I am with all of that. But we have to go let Mooch out first."

Right. The dog.

Caleb blew out a breath. "Let's go then."

Moving fast, they walked hand-in-hand across the lawn to her house, circling through the gate to the back door.

"Is he going to scratch at the door the whole time trying to get into the bedroom?"

Emerson reached for the knob. "I have no idea. I think if I hook him up with a rawhide he'll—The door's unlocked."

Alarm cut through the simmering lust. He moved her away from the door. "Stay out here."

"I'm coming with you."

"Emerson—"

"That's my dog in there," she insisted.

Understanding warred with the need to protect her. "Then stay behind me."

When she nodded, he eased open the door and listened. No sound of canine feet on the wood floors. No indication of anyone else. They moved inside. In the dim light from the stove and the single lamp from the front entryway, it didn't appear as if anything had been disturbed. The TV and electronics were still there, and nothing seemed out of place in the kitchen. He edged down the hall, toward the stairs, aware of Emerson at his back.

Something moved on the second floor and he tensed, bracing for a fight. He'd keep her safe, whatever it took.

Mooch trotted down the stairs, tags jingling, butt wagging. He made a beeline for Emerson, who crouched down to rub his head.

Caleb blew out a breath, relieved the dog was okay. "He probably wouldn't be so chill if there was an actual intruder. Maybe you left the door unlocked?"

"You watched me lock it."

Yeah, he'd totally thought he had, but in truth, he'd been more focused on imagining peeling her out of that dress, so he couldn't say with certainty.

Recognizing she wouldn't be easy until he'd checked the whole house, he curled his hands around her shoulders. "Take Mooch on out. I'll sweep the rest of the house."

The door at the top of the stairs swung open. Emerson shrieked. Someone else screamed, and Caleb instantly leapt to protect, shielding her with his body.

"Auntie Em?"

Fiona. It was Fiona standing at the top of the landing.

Caleb relaxed, dropping his head back against the wall as the adrenaline dump made his limbs shake.

Emerson clutched her chest, as if that would stop the heart no doubt trying to pound out of it. "Holy mother of God, child. I didn't know you'd come home. You scared the life out of me."

She'd obviously been sleeping. Pillow marks creased her cheeks. But her face was puffy, too, as if she'd been crying.

Caleb narrowed his eyes. "You okay, kid?"

Fiona's lip wobbled and she swiped a hand under her nose. "Boys are stupid."

"Unquestionably. Do I need to kill anybody?" If some punkass college boy had hurt her... "I can probably tag a couple of probies to help me hide a body if I have to."

She offered up a tremulous smile. "No. But thank you for the offer."

"I'm gonna let Mooch out and make some tea, okay? Then you can tell us what happened."

Caleb liked that "us" a helluva lot. She wasn't kicking him out to do the parenting thing, wasn't taking it all on herself. He understood what that meant for Emerson, who never asked for help. It made him feel damned good to be included.

"I'll be down in a minute."

He trailed Emerson downstairs and put on the kettle himself as she let the dog out. It was probably a good thing Fi had left the door unlocked. Much as he wanted her to know about them, he didn't want her finding out by walking in on him getting Emerson naked.

*Oh hey kiddo. I know I promised you I'd look out for your godmother. You totally meant giving her as many orgasms as possible, right?*

Yeah, that was not the kind of awkward he wanted to deal with.

Emerson joined him at the stove, trailing a light hand down his arm. "Sorry about this," she murmured.

"It's fine. There's time." It wouldn't be the first night he had only himself and his right hand for relief.

Fiona padded in and slumped onto one of the barstools at the counter. Emerson moved to pull out mugs and tea, automatically prepping each of their favorites.

"Have you eaten?" Caleb asked.

Fi shook her head, looking miserable.

He moved to the freezer, checking the ice cream stash.

"What are you doing?"

"I had a lot of sisters. I know that face. It calls for ice cream." Plunking the carton on the counter, he dug out a scoop and bowl. "So who is he and how bad did he screw up?"

"His name is Corbin."

Emerson's hands paused on the kettle. "Your lab partner in astronomy?"

Fi's shoulders hunched. "Yeah."

"I thought you two were just friends." Emerson's carefully neutral tone had Caleb wondering whether he needed to worry.

"I mean, we are. Good friends. We've got so much in common, and we've been hanging out a lot since the start of school. But we keep having these sort of...almost moments. You know?"

Enough of those almost moments built up to certainty. Caleb couldn't stop himself from glancing at Emerson. "Yeah. I get you. So you think there's something more than friendship there?"

"I mean...yeah. But he keeps doing this kind of hot-cold thing. Not, like, mean. Just, like, pretending the moments aren't happening."

Oh, how familiar this sounded. Not that he necessarily thought Fi should take his tactic of kissing the hell out of her friend.

Emerson set a mug in front of Fi. "Are you worried you're misreading the situation, baby?"

Fiona frowned and poked at her ice cream. "No. I just...Last night, when we were doing our lab work, he nearly kissed me. But then he pulled back and made this lame excuse like that wasn't what he was doing."

Emerson scowled. "You've got enough on your plate, and you deserve better than a bunch of hot and cold from someone. He sounds like he's either high maintenance or doesn't know what he wants."

If he hadn't known what Emerson had been through, Caleb would've stared at her. There was no question that her lousy track record with her ex was coloring her advice. But they could do better. He turned his attention back to Fi. "What are you getting out of this friendship?"

"I mean...friendship. We're close. We confide in each other. I'm the first person he calls with news. He's my go-to person when I want to hang out or go do something. We're each other's cheerleader, you know?"

Color bloomed in Emerson's cheeks as she wrapped her hands

around her own mug. "Yeah, that makes sense." The gaze she cast toward him was full of emotion. Oh yeah, she understood that's what he'd done. What he'd keep doing.

But this wasn't about them.

Caleb bumped Fiona's shoulder. "The fact is, if it makes you feel good to connect with this guy—on whatever level—then maybe it's worth whatever rough patches you go through on the way to figuring out whatever you're going to be to each other."

"Yeah. And I'd be fine just being besties. At least, I think I would. I'd just like to know, one way or the other, you know?"

Caleb totally knew. Just as he knew that now they'd crossed this line, he couldn't go back with Emerson.

"Sometimes it takes people a long time to get up the guts to admit what they want. Especially if what they want changes something they already value." Emerson kept her focus on her daughter, but Caleb knew she spoke to him.

He wished they could do more of this. They'd rock this co-parenting thing for their own child.

As the thought struck him, Caleb instinctively pulled back, remembering their conversation about kids when Fi left for college. Emerson considered herself done with that phase of life. If that wasn't something she wanted, he didn't want to let himself go down the path of dreaming about it himself. She was absolutely enough, all on her own.

But as Fiona continued to talk, Emerson met his gaze across the island, her expression full of shared amusement and gratitude, he thought of her epiphany at dinner. That she wasn't old. Wasn't some kind of cougar. Maybe there was a chance she'd change her mind.

# CHAPTER 9

*D*espite all her intentions to start sleeping in once Fiona left for college, years of habit had Emerson rising early for that first cup of coffee on the back deck, knowing it was the only stretch of the day she could reliably get quiet outside the recording booth with her talky teen in residence. She felt a snap in the air as she stepped out, mug clutched in her hands. Autumn was coming, and she couldn't wait. While Mooch raced down to the yard to do his business, she moved to the rail on Caleb's side, also out of long habit. How many mornings had she found him out there, too, enjoying the calm before he headed in to work? She wondered now if that was his own preference or if he'd done it hoping to see her.

He'd gone home alone last night, their plans having been ruined yet again by teenager interruptus. Age epiphanies aside, this was still her life. Fiona still had to come first. But for the first time in a long time, Emerson wanted to put in the effort to carve out some space for herself, for something beyond being a parent. She wanted to carve out space for Caleb, more than the habitual ways he'd integrated into their lives over the past few years.

The sound of a door opening pulled her attention to his back porch. And there he was, stepping out in basketball shorts and a t-shirt that clung to his muscled chest. His gaze instantly found hers and those lips she'd come to love curved into a smile.

Emerson held up a finger to him and went back inside to pour a second cup of coffee with a splash of cream, just the way he liked it. Then she walked over, her faithful shadow on her heels.

"I come bearing caffeine."

"My second favorite thing to see in the morning." He accepted the mug and pulled her in with one arm for a soft kiss that had all her lingering tension melting away. "Hi."

"Mmm, that might be better than coffee."

"Might? I clearly need to work on my technique." Setting his mug down, he sank into a chair, pulling her into a sprawl across his lap.

It seemed the most natural thing in the world to snuggle against him, resting her head on his shoulder. "I feel like you just need more opportunity to practice. I'm sorry about last night."

Mooch circled three times before flopping down at their feet with a heavy sigh.

Caleb banded his arm around her waist, sliding his hand beneath the hem of her shirt and settling warm fingers against her skin before reaching for his coffee. "I didn't mind. Not really. I like being able to help out with Fiona. I always have."

"It was nice knowing you had my back. You'd make a really good father."

The moment the words were out of her mouth, she wished she could take them back. This was off the map, off their charted course. Here there be thought monsters that could screw this whole thing up. But it had been on her mind all night, and her uncaffeinated brain had run away with her. Again.

He didn't tense up, but he noticed she had. "That weirds you out."

"No. Yes. I don't know. Part and parcel of that whole epiphany I had about my age last night was thinking about how, if Fi hadn't come to me and I'd been in a committed enough relationship for kids at the time, my kid would only be three. We'd be still in diapers or potty training or whatever. I don't even know what age that happens. And that's so weird for me to think of because I just sort of naturally felt like, oh that part of my life is done because my kid just graduated high school. And last night reminded me that it's not. That the life I wanted before isn't off the table."

That was both wonderful and terrifying.

"What did you want, exactly?"

She hesitated, almost afraid to give voice to it. But this was Caleb. He wouldn't judge her, and it was easier to say while not looking him in the face.

"Marriage. Family. I wanted all those milestones and firsts without the burden of grief. I wanted to build the family I didn't have growing up. After Fi, I just couldn't imagine it. And we built our own family."

He said nothing, continuing to sip his coffee and stroke the strip of skin at her waist, as if he sensed there was more she wanted to say.

"Is that something you want?" She was getting way ahead of things. But she needed to know what he had in mind so she could manage her own expectations. Was this a fun affair or an audition for the long-term? Did she want it to be more than the fun?

"I always figured I'd get married eventually. Have kids. But I've got a pretty flexible definition of family." He sipped at the coffee. "You know I lost my folks in a car crash when I was about Fi's age. I didn't have someone like you to take me on, so I ended up in the foster system. My experience there was better than most. My foster mom, Joan, was a powerhouse. She had a way of making everyone family. And with all the kids going in and out of her care, we had a big one."

Realization dawned. "That's how you and Kyle are brothers. You were foster brothers."

"Yeah. He's one of many. After losing my parents, feeling like I had no one, it was pretty damned amazing to find that. Even the kids who were there temporarily were made to feel part of the family. That was Joan's gift, one that's kept on giving long after we left her."

"She sounds wonderful."

"She was." His voice hitched, just a little. "She died in a car accident herself a couple years ago. Black ice."

Emerson straightened to look at him, noting the hints of grief in his eyes. "Caleb. I had no idea. Why didn't you tell me you were dealing with this?"

She slid her arms around him, wanting to comfort, even though the hurt wasn't exactly new. He'd so often been her rock, and she found she wanted to be the same for him.

He wrapped her in his arms and shrugged. "I grieved with my family. And I liked being able to come back and spend time with you and Fiona, without that hanging over the whole thing. I didn't want to remind either of you of the accident."

Not knowing what else to do, she pressed a kiss to his temple.

"Joan would have liked you a lot, and she'd have adored Fi."

"That feels like a pretty amazing compliment." Relaxing again, she absorbed the comfortable feel of being in his arms. "This whole interlude has felt like a pretty amazing way to start the day."

"I'd say the only way to beat it would be waking up next to you with enough time for a little morning delight."

His words woke the lust she'd managed to bank late into the night. "Mmm. Can't argue with that. Sadly, we probably won't get that alone time until after your next shift. Fiona decided to stay until Sunday night, so I figured I'd jump ahead on the schedule as much as I can, squeeze in some booth time before she gets up. I wish we had a little more flexibility."

"Me, too." He brushed his lips over hers in another quiet, drugging kiss, underscored with promises. "But I need you to know, as much as I want you, I want this, too. The quiet mornings. The talking. I want it all, Em."

As his dark eyes searched hers, her heart leapt into her throat. This felt like so much more than quiet mornings and talking. It felt like everything she hadn't known she was still waiting for.

Emerson couldn't quite let herself believe in that. Not yet. They were too new. This thing between them was still fresh and heady and full of quagmires they had yet to face. Right now they were still in the fantasy stage. Who knew where it would take them? But the prospect of a true future of that everything with him felt like a lovely, waking dream, one she hugged to her heart as she kissed him goodbye and crossed back to her house to start the day.

* * *

ANOTHER SHIFT DOWN. The next three days were free and clear, and Caleb had specific and detailed plans for how he wanted to spend all of them. Or as much as he could manage around Emerson's work schedule. Flowers in hand and an everlasting chew toy in a bag for Mooch, he crossed the yard and headed for her back door.

Finding it unlocked he pushed it open. "Honey, I'm—"

"Help!"

For a moment, Caleb could only stare at the chaos. Mooch stood in the middle of the kitchen table, having narrowly missed a centerpiece of flowers and thankfully unlit candles. Something on the stove was smoking, and water fountained up from the sink. He didn't even see Emerson.

*Holy shit.*

Dropping the flowers and chew toy on the table by the door, he bolted into the kitchen, sloshing through the water covering the tile floor. The contents of the cabinet under the sink were scattered on the floor, and Emerson was twisted half in, half out of the space.

"I can't get the damned water shut off!"

Caleb grabbed her by the waist and dragged her out, reaching for the wrench in her hand. "Why the hell do you have a pipe wrench?"

"Because the knob broke off!"

"Where's the main shutoff to the house?"

"In the front yard but locked so only the water department can access it. Apparently whoever built the house didn't see fit to have a main shutoff besides that."

Hunkering down, he immediately got soaked as he managed to get the wrench on what remained of the shutoff valve and crank. The geyser of water stopped. Edging out of the cabinet, he straightened. "Well, that was unexpected."

Emerson's expression was grim, as if she'd been waging war. Which, he supposed, she had. Her hair hung in wet ropes and makeup ran down her face. She wore a dress and an apron, both drenched.

*Oh damn.*

Before he could think of something comforting to say, the fire alarm went off.

"Son of a bitch!" She twisted off the heat on the stove and shoved the smoking pot aside, stalking in bare feet to throw open the back door for the smoke to dissipate. "Off the table."

Mooch looked at her as if she was nuts.

"Off! Go outside."

He leapt neatly down, managing to avoid the worst of the water, and made a beeline for the back yard.

For a moment, she simply stood there, breathing hard. Her gaze landed on the flowers he'd tossed. Some choked, pained noise seemed to catch in her throat. When she lifted her gaze back to his, her chin trembled and those big blue eyes swam with unshed tears. "Maybe this is a sign."

Caleb snapped into gear, striding over to grip her by the shoulders. "It's not a sign. Go change clothes and dry off. I'm going to start mopping up down here. Spare towels in the laundry room?"

She sniffed. "There are more in the linen closet upstairs. I'll bring them down. It's probably going to take every single one."

Knowing he had his work cut out for him to salvage the night, he dove in. By the time she came back down in dry clothes, face washed, with her hair twisted up, the smoke alarm had stopped shrieking, and he'd retrieved the shop vac from his place. He'd already used up every towel on the first floor.

"The good news is your wood floors aren't ruined. The bad news...you need a new shutoff valve and apparently a new faucet."

She began to scatter her armful of towels and sheets to soak up the remaining water. "You forgot to mention the scorched and completely inedible dinner."

Yeah, he'd been hoping she'd forget about that.

"I was trying to do something romantic. I suppose I should be grateful I hadn't gotten around to lighting the candles. Mooch probably would have knocked them over, and then you'd have had to work tonight, either way."

Stepping into her path, Caleb cupped her face. "We'll go pick up the parts. They're easy replacements. And we'll grab takeout on the way. I know it's not what you planned, but it'll be fine."

"It's just another disaster. One of these days, you're going to get sick of rescuing me from them."

"Never." He pressed a quick kiss to her lips. "And it's not another disaster. It's just life. Relationships aren't only about the good stuff. They're about the messy stuff, too. C'mon. Let's finish cleaning up the worst of this and hit up Home Depot."

He'd managed to mostly pull Emerson out of her funk by the time they made it to the plumbing aisle.

"I think you're really going to dig the new faucet. That tall goose neck will be a lot easier to use than what you had before. We've just got to find the shutoff valves, and we're good to go."

A man further down the aisle looked up. "They're down here."

"Oh, thanks, man."

As they got closer, the guy frowned. "It's Caleb, right?"

He focused in, knowing he recognized the face but not quite able to place it.

"Wyatt Sullivan. We met last year at Joan's funeral."

The lightbulb went off. "Right. Sure. You were one of the adoptees that predated me."

Something flickered over Wyatt's face. "Yeah. I'd been gone a long time, but you never really forget your time with Joan."

"True enough. I didn't realize you lived in Hamilton."

"I sort of bounce around, living wherever my current flip is. I'm a contractor. Flipping houses is what I do for a living."

"You're DIWyatt," Emerson announced.

Caleb glanced down at her. "He's what now?"

"DIWyatt. He's got this whole channel on YouTube with episodes on how to do home improvement stuff. My friend Paisley is a big fan."

"Oh yeah? Is she into home improvement?" Wyatt asked.

Her lips quirked, her eyes sparking with the first hint of humor Caleb had seen all night. "She's into men in tool belts."

"Ah." Clearly at a loss for how to reply, Wyatt rocked back on his heels. "Are you going to the family reunion in a few weeks?"

Caleb had been so tied up with Emerson, he hadn't even thought about it. But the idea of getting out of town, taking her with him to meet the family definitely held some appeal. And maybe, if they managed to get out of town, they'd break this streak of interruptions at every turn.

"Haven't decided yet. Kinda depends on work."

"I hear that. I'm hoping to be done with my flip. Maybe I'll see you there."

"Yeah, maybe so. It was good to see you again. We gotta get home to fix a kitchen sink."

"You need any help, let me know." He dug out a card and passed it over.

"Appreciate it, man. You have a good night."

They made it back to Emerson's without further incident. After fueling themselves with bucket chicken and biscuits, of which Mooch only managed to beg a tiny piece, they had another hunt for a secondary shutoff valve to the main water line. Caleb finally managed to locate it under the deck. Knowing she'd feel better once everything was done, he dove in. Like all home repair projects, it took longer than they wanted. But hours after he'd showed up, he turned the water back on and tested the new faucet.

"Good as new," he pronounced. "And didn't even need to call in family favors."

"Joan's kids get around, don't they?"

"She was a foster parent for twenty-five years. She helped a lot of kids." He hesitated, shutting off the faucet and starting to gather up tools. "Would you like to meet some of them?"

Emerson studied him. "You want them to meet me?"

He couldn't take her to meet his parents, but this—showing her where he came from—felt important. "Yeah. The girls—Joan's actual adopted daughters—are keeping up the tradition of an annual reunion of former fosters. They've turned the house into an inn and spa. We could go. Have a weekend away, just the two of us."

Her smile was wry. "You sure you want to risk going anywhere with me? We could end up with multiple flat tires. Or run out of gas. Or be beamed up by aliens. That's starting to feel not outside the realm of possibilities for interruptions."

Closing the toolbox, he slid his arms around her, lacing his hands at the small of her back. "There is nobody I'd rather have flat tires or run out of gas or face down little green men with than you."

"You're sweet. And yes, I'd love to go. We might finally manage to make it to bed if we're out of town."

He angled his head, studying the tired lines of her face. It was beyond late. He could let it go. But he had a feeling that if he let another night go by, she'd start finding ways to convince herself that there really was some kind of cosmic plan to keep them apart, and he didn't want to lose ground.

"The night's not over yet."

Her brows drew together in consternation. "But everything was ruined. Dinner. My outfit. You had to do plumbing, Caleb. That's not a date."

"I got to spend the evening with you, so as far as I'm concerned, nothing important got ruined."

"I wanted everything to be perfect." Her lip rolled out just a little in a pout.

Caleb nipped it gently. "You're here. I'm here. The flood was averted. That's all the perfection I need, Emerson. Let me take you to bed."

# CHAPTER 10

*D*espite Paisley's lecture, Emerson's doubts had festered for days. Worry that all the interruptions and chaos were simply a precursor to the inevitable. That she wouldn't be enough. That she'd somehow disappoint him. She'd wanted all the trappings of romance, all the things she'd thought she could control, so that there'd be something to distract from her imperfections. The thighs that still jiggled more than she wanted. The breasts that weren't quite as pert as they used to be, with one a little smaller than the other.

But she hadn't been able to control anything. Every single effort had gone straight to hell. The perfection she'd been chasing clearly didn't actually exist. Not for them.

As she stared up at the naked yearning in Caleb's eyes, she understood he meant every word. He didn't need perfect. He just wanted her.

Would that ever stop seeming like a miracle?

He skimmed his fingers over her cheek. "Do you want me to go?"

She could only shake her head. This wouldn't be the frantic, mindless passion she'd imagined. This was something else. Something that scared her more than a little. But she didn't have it in her to turn him away. "Stay."

His lips curved before he lowered them to hers for a long, drugging kiss that made her forget about the plumbing and the flooding and the ruined dinner. She couldn't hold on to anything but the taste of him as his mouth opened over hers, seducing her into languid compliance.

Before he could shut down the last of her brain cells, she eased back. "We should try for a bed this time."

"I'm on it." Releasing her, he crossed to the back door, pulling something out of a bag she only just now noticed. "Hey buddy. Hey, Mooch. You want a treat?"

At the magic word, her dog perked up, scrambling off his bed in the living room and dancing at Caleb's feet, until he brought a big round thing out of the bag.

"What is that?"

"Allegedly, it's an everlasting dog treat. The ball itself is supposed to be nigh indestructible, and the treat compartment is refillable. I'm hoping it'll keep him distracted for a while."

"Have I mentioned that your penchant for thinking ahead is a really attractive characteristic?"

"I'm extremely motivated." He led Mooch back over to his bed. "Lay down. That's a good boy. Here you go."

Mooch's nose twitched as he investigated the toy, then looked back at her.

"It's okay, baby. That's for you. You can have it."

Stub tail wagging, he began to gnaw.

They made it upstairs without being followed. As he stepped into her room, she shut the door, leaning back against it with a sigh of relief. "Mission accomplished."

His gaze slid over the space. Here, at least, things weren't chaos. Other than the discarded dress and apron that trailed out of the hamper, nothing out of place. She'd planned for tonight. The bed was made up with clean, soft sheets, and candles were scattered on the dresser and side tables. Caleb picked up the lighter on the nightstand and began to set them to flame.

Emerson stayed where she was, watching him. He'd never been up here before. The room felt smaller with him in it, a big man moving with purpose through her space, setting the mood she'd wanted. She liked seeing him here. Liked knowing she'd soon have him in her bed. Over her. Under her. Inside her. And the knowing made her heartbeat quicken.

He came back to her, the flickering glow casting his face in semi-shadow. She'd chosen candles more for the flattering lighting than for romance, but he was looking at her, in her damp t-shirt and old jeans, as if she were Helen of Troy. Anxious again, she tensed against the door.

She was no goddess. She was just Emerson.

Cupping her face in his work-roughened hands, Caleb took her under with more of those languorous kisses, until the nerves abated and his clever hands had stripped her down to nothing but the lacy bikini briefs.

"Oh, I really like these." He slid one finger just inside the waistband, skimming along the elastic and sparking awareness along her belly and lower.

Emerson's breath hitched. "Really? I was thinking they were awful and really needed to go."

On a low chuckle, he scooped her up and carried her to the bed. The mattress dipped beneath his weight as he joined her. His mouth came back to hers, and she reached for the hem of his shirt, tugging it up.

"You're getting a bit behind here, Caleb."

Reaching back with one hand, he tugged it off and tossed it to the floor. "I'm right on schedule." He began to kiss and stroke his way down her body, lighting little fires along every inch. "I made you a promise the other night. I intend to keep it."

Emerson's breath hitched as he began to slowly drag her underwear down. She'd replayed those heated words from his truck over and over, imagining, anticipating exactly this. Her imagination had let her down. The sight of Caleb's big, broad shoulders between her legs, his hooded eyes taking her in with a reverent curse was better than any fantasy. Slipping his hands beneath her, he dragged her closer and rubbed one stubbled cheek along the sensitive skin of her inner thighs. Just the rasp of it almost sent her over the edge.

"So fucking beautiful. I've wanted you for so damned long, Emerson. I've dreamed about how you'd taste, how you'd feel. I'm not going to be in a rush here."

"When I die of anticipation, it'll be on your head," she managed.

Chuckling, he closed his mouth over her.

On a gasp, she bowed up off the bed as the stunning pleasure whipped through her. He just used his hands to pin her in place as he drove her completely out of her mind with slow, ruthless precision. He made her scream, and after the first brutal orgasm, he whipped her to a frenzy again, until she was limp and gasping, hoarse from begging and cursing him. Only then did he strip out of the last of his clothes, roll on a condom, and crawl up her body, settling in the cradle of her hips.

He paused there, his heavy cock nudging her entrance. "You okay?"

"I'm pretty sure you killed me and this is the afterlife. But maybe you'd better try again to be absolutely certain." She figured death by orgasm was a pretty great way to go. Paisley would definitely approve.

He was grinning, his eyes full of warmth and affection as he began to slide inside her. She held that gaze as it sharpened, as her body stretched around him, until the humor fell away and she was so deliciously full of him, she had to close her eyes in an effort to hold onto every moment of pleasure.

She'd wanted perfect, and this was it. He was it. Impossible. Improbable. Hers.

"Look at me."

At the unmistakable order, she opened her eyes, focusing on his face as he hovered above her, noting the mix of fierce concentration and tenderness. Needing closer, she arched up, taking his mouth and squeezing her legs tighter around his hips to pull him deeper. Deeper. Until he was buried to the hilt.

Caleb shuddered, dropping his brow to hers as he groaned her name. He began to move. With every slow, deliberate stroke, it felt as if he stripped away her defenses. But she couldn't look away, couldn't stop the exquisite sensation of being taken by him, cared for by him. Sex had never been this good before. And as they crested the peak together, she knew it never would be with anyone else again.

* * *

CALEB WOKE TIRED AND HAPPY.

Emerson let him stay. He hadn't expected that. But sometime after round three, they'd both essentially passed out. In truth, judging by the sun slanting across the foot of the bed, that hadn't been all that many hours ago. Now she slept tucked up against him, exactly where she belonged. They'd need to get up soon, let out the dog, start their day. But he didn't want to budge from his position as big spoon. Not yet.

Last night had been...everything. Even with the plumbing disaster. Or maybe because of it. That probably made him a perverse bastard, but he liked the domesticity of it. There'd been no pretension, no artifice of special occasions or romance. Just real life that had bled straight into raw needs and wants. They were incredible together in bed, eager and insatiable. But they were equally good out of it. He enjoyed taking care of Emerson and loved that she was starting to let him. They fit on every level, exactly as he'd known they would. It was so easy to imagine what it would be like to be by her side for every day, not just when they could carve out time. A unit.

God, he wanted that.

Now that he had her, it was so damned hard not to reach for everything. She'd left the starting line but she was still a long damned way from the final stretch. Patience was vital at this stage. He wasn't playing the short game here. He was in it for the long haul. The certainty of that gave him pause. Maybe on some level he'd always known Emerson was it for him. It was why he'd bought the house, wasn't it? To be closer to her, make her a part of his world in the only way he could? He'd earned her friendship, her trust, and now her intimacy. As she stirred, stretching against him so his cock was nestled firmly against her backside, Caleb told himself he could be content with that. For now.

At the testing flex of his hips, she arched further on a sleepy moan, and he found her already wet. Yeah, he could definitely be content with this. Palming her breast, he slipped through her folds, slowly working his crown against her clit.

"Inside me, " she murmured.

He started to obey, sliding one precious inch inside her tight, wet heat before he froze.

"Don't stop."

"Condom," he choked.

"It's fine. IUD."

Caleb didn't move. He'd never been with a woman without protection. Had never wanted to risk it. But this was Emerson. His Emerson. If ever there was someone he wanted to take that risk with, it was her.

"Sure?"

In answer, she pressed back, taking him in.

Perfect. She felt so fucking perfect. They moved together in a lazy, easy rhythm, drawing out the pleasure of the slow rise. Every day. He wanted to start his day making love to this woman every day for the rest of his life. The thought of it had his balls tightening on the edge of release. Holding on to his last sliver of control, he slipped his fingers between her legs, circling her clit, until he felt her walls begin to flutter around him. Losing the battle, he surged into her one last time and emptied himself in wave after wave of pleasure.

They lay quiet for a long time after. Was she as wrecked as he was? He sure as hell hoped he wasn't the only one this far gone.

"You were right," she rasped.

"About?"

"This is definitely better than coffee."

He rumbled a laugh, rousing himself to press a kiss to her bare shoulder. "After that, I might sell my soul for coffee and some kind of food."

"Given I lost count of the orgasms last night, I feel like the least I can do is feed you." She patted his arm, and he could hear the smile in her voice. "We have to keep up your strength."

"I really love how insatiable you are."

"I really love that you can keep up with me."

*I really love you.*

But he held the words in, knowing it was too soon. Instead, he released her and rolled out of bed to retrieve a towel. With a playful snap, he tossed it at her. "C'mon, woman. Get moving. You promised me breakfast."

After a quick clean up, they opened the door to head downstairs and all but tripped over Mooch, who'd taken up position as a rug in the hallway. He hadn't made a peep all night. At their appearance, he bounced to his feet and raced down the stairs.

"I've got him. You get coffee." Trotting down after the dog, Caleb opened the back door and let him out.

When he came back in, Emerson was moving around the kitchen in nothing but his shirt. Damn but he loved that.

Enjoying the view, he kicked back against the counter while she measured grounds. "So you answered a question of mine last night."

"Oh? What was that?"

"I've listened to all these books you've narrated, including all the sexy parts, and I always wondered if that's how you really sounded when you came."

She went brows up. "And?"

"It's different."

"Well, I'd hope it would be different from the best sex of my life."

Caleb couldn't hold back the smug grin. "The best, huh?"

"I mean, you were there, so..." She shrugged, unabashed. "Stroking your ego at this point seems superfluous."

More than satisfied with that, he snagged her around the waist and tugged her close, skimming a hand up the back of her thigh to squeeze her bare ass. "Just out of curiosity, have you ever...you know...when recording one of those scenes?"

On a snort, she batted his hand away and moved to the sink. "No way. That mic picks up the barest stomach noises. There's no *way* I could or would do *that*. That would be totally weird. It's a *When Harry Met Sally* all the way."

"A what?"

"You know, when Meg Ryan's character gets into that argument with Billy Crystal about women faking orgasms and she does right there in the middle of the diner?"

At a loss, he just stared at her.

"You have no idea what I'm talking about."

"I do not."

She dumped the water in and started the coffeemaker. "Oh my God, I keep forgetting you're a baby."

"Not a baby, just not up on classic romantic comedies."

"You're getting a movie-cation. A movie-vention? Whatever, I'm totally making you watch it."

"Can we watch it from bed?" A guy could hope.

"No. Because I want you to actually watch it, not try to distract me with amazing sex."

"I didn't hear you complaining last night."

"I was not trying to fill in a gap in your pop culture knowledge last night." She winced as she bent to grab eggs out of the fridge. "Besides, if you have your wicked way with me any more today, I don't think I'll be able to walk."

Caleb prowled over, sliding his arms around her from behind and nuzzling her neck. "You'll just have to fulfill some of my other fantasies then."

"Mmm. You checked off several of mine last night, so it's only fair."

"I've already gotten a pretty good start on the list."

"There's a list?"

"Oh yeah. I've been working on it for a while."

"What fantasies are we talking about?" The tone of her voice proved she was expecting the salacious kind. After the books he'd listened to, he had plenty of those stored up, too. But that wasn't what he wanted just now.

"I want to cook breakfast with you. Then, I want to clean up and take you on a tour of all the best street art of Nashville. I wanna get ice cream at Jeni's. And then I want to come back and curl up with you for a nap because I figure that's about as far as the cumulative endorphins and sugar will take us before we crash."

Very gently, she set down the egg in her hand. "Those are your fantasies?"

He cuddled her closer. "I'm basically getting my fantasy every day I'm with you. I've never been happier. So yeah, those are my fantasies. For today, anyway."

Sensing he'd flummoxed her, he aimed for a little teasing. "I mean, I'd prefer to clean up in the same shower, but we've gotta protect your ability to walk for the tour. It's a sacrifice I'm willing to make, if you are."

When she said nothing, a kernel of worry lodged in his gut. Had he pushed too far after all?

On a sigh, she pivoted in his embrace and slid her arms around his waist, resting her head against his shoulder. "I've never been happier either."

Pressing a kiss to her temple, he crossed another thing off his list.

# CHAPTER 11

*'I really like your mouth.'*

*Aaron gave a strangled laugh and dropped his temple to hers. 'Don't say stuff like that. It makes me want to use it on every inch of you.'*

*'Oh, God.' Gemma closed her eyes and rode out the blast of lust that shot through her. 'Don't say stuff like that. It makes me want to let you.'*

*'How do you want to proceed with this?' he asked.*

Straight to your bed. Do not pass Go, do not collect $200. *She swallowed. 'Carefully, I think. Very carefully.'*"

Satisfied with the take, Emerson stopped recording, saved the file, and tugged off her headphones. One more session ought to get this one done. But first, a break with Mooch and maybe a snack.

Flipping the switch that controlled the *On Air* light outside, she opened the door to her recording booth. A glorified closet lined in acoustic foam, there was barely room for her computer, microphone, a stand to hold the iPad she used for scripts, and her shelf of moisturizing agents—eye drops, nose drops, lip balm, bottle of water—so her faithful pup always took up a position right outside. Mooch scrambled up from his post, ecstatic to see her as always. That never got old.

"Hey baby boy. Want to go outside?"

He wagged his butt and danced toward the stairs. In the kitchen, she snagged a fresh bottle of water and the phone she'd left on the counter, and headed out back so Mooch could have a run. He clattered down the deck stairs and began to pounce at the early autumn leaves that had begun to fall. How the hell was it already mid-October?

Swiping open her phone, she checked her messages.

Her heart gave a happy bump at the stack of texts from Caleb on the screen.

**Hey gorgeous. Miss you.**

She missed him, too. Missed having him in her bed. Not just for the sex—although, hell yes—but because she actually loved sleeping with him. Waking up with him wrapped around her was becoming her favorite indulgence. It seemed impossible that she'd already gotten used to having him there. Maybe she should've been concerned at the ease with which they'd fallen into sleepovers, but there was no question this thing between them wasn't remotely a casual fling.

She really, really had to find a way to tell Fiona about them. But Fi had been wrapped up in school, headed for midterms, and Emerson had just...let it slide. When she was with Caleb, it was easy to fall into the fantasy that it was just the two of them. After their trip to Eden's Ridge for the family reunion this weekend, she'd just have to rip the Band-aid off and be prepared for the fallout.

Resolved, she scanned the rest of the text thread.

**I forgot my phone charger. If you've got time when you're on a break between sessions, could you bring it to me at the station?**

For a chance to see him for a few minutes? Yeah, she could totally do that. Glancing down at her ancient yoga pants and the t-shirt of his she'd totally stolen, she considered she should probably change first. And brush her hair. Not that he cared one way or the other, but there was that whole going out in public thing. Leaving Mooch to his leaves, she went to make herself presentable.

Forty-five minutes later, she arrived at the fire station to find the yard overrun with tiny humans in red plastic fire helmets. Two firefighters were at the center of a circle, one of them in full turnout gear, the other obviously explaining things to the audience of children and the flanking ring of moms. Instantly recognizing Caleb as the one in the gear, she pulled off to the side of the lot and edged over to watch, not wanting to interrupt.

"This right here is called an SCBA," Darren—otherwise known as Showboat—explained. "That's a self-contained breathing apparatus. This is how we breathe in a fire."

Caleb adjusted something and spoke. "It makes me sound kind of scary, but it's still just me inside. Nothing to be afraid of or hide from. If you're in a fire and you see somebody dressed like us, we're there to help you."

As Darren went over some more rules of fire safety, Caleb began to strip his gear back off.

One of the children crawled forward to tug on his pants leg.

Caleb dropped down to one knee, getting on the boy's level. Something about his intent focus on the child made Emerson's heart turn over. Judging by a few of the sighs she overheard from the moms, she wasn't the only one.

"When there's a fire, y'all have to get dressed real fast, don't you?"

"Sure do."

"Like…how fast?"

Caleb flashed a grin. "How about we have a little competition to find out?"

"Yeah!" the kids cheered.

"Okay. I'm gonna strip back down. Y'all pick which firefighter you want to race me."

"I'd like to watch him strip down," one of the moms muttered.

*It's a helluva show.* But Emerson kept that to herself.

In the end, the kids voted on Peach and divided into teams supporting their preferred firefighter. One of the other guys—Roadie, she thought—stood in the middle, acting as emcee. He held a stopwatch in his hand.

"We go on three. Can y'all count with me? One." All the little voices joined in. "Two. Three!"

The kids roared their approval, cheering on their chosen competitor. The pair of them flew, hands almost a blur as they stepped into pants and boots, layered on headgear, and shrugged on coats.

Emerson couldn't stop herself from joining in the cheers. "Go! Go! Go! You've got it, Torch!"

Caleb fumbled the belt clasp on his SCBA, his head jerking in her direction. Oops. A ripple of laugher went through the rest of his company as Peach shot into the lead. Caleb got instantly back with it, but there was no catching up. Peach jerked on her gloves and pumped her fists in victory a full two seconds before he did.

"We have a winner! 41.96 seconds!"

In the wake of the competition, the kids got redirected to practicing stop-drop-and-roll on the grass. Several of the moms congregated to the side as Peach and Caleb slipped out of their gear.

"You think we could get a special adults only show of the reverse of that process?" one murmured.

"In slow motion," another added.

"Maybe with a hose."

As Caleb broke away from the group and headed their way, Emerson couldn't help but agree with them. She knew exactly how good his bare chest looked when wet.

With a polite nod at the women, he crossed straight over to her. "Hey, babe."

"Sorry about the distraction. I got carried away with the sense of competition."

"Worth it." He brushed a chaste kiss over her lips and took the charger she offered. "Thanks for bringing this by."

"Did you really need it, or was it just an excuse to see me?"

"Both."

"I was happy to come by either way."

"Sorry I can't visit." He jerked his head back toward the kids. "I gotta get back to this."

"Mind if I stick around to watch?"

"Sure. Stay as long as you like. If you play your cards right, you might get an invite to dinner. Fonzie's making chili."

"Is that a good thing or a bad thing?"

"You have a cast iron stomach and love all things spicy. You'll be fine."

"Noted. I can't really stay that long, though. I've still got work to finish up."

"Fair enough. You'll be ready to go when I get off work tomorrow? I'd like to get on the road as early as possible"

"With bells on. We'll just need to drop Mooch off with Paisley on our way out of town." Because she sensed the mom group staring, she couldn't quite resist leaning in to kiss him again, lingering just a shade too long for polite company. "Thanks for making my day."

He winked, totally onto what she was doing. "Any time, pretty lady."

She stuck around at the periphery, watching him interact with the kids through the tour of the trucks. He was a natural. She'd seen it in how he interacted with Fiona, but this was different. He didn't talk down to them, didn't get impatient. He treated them as exactly what they were—little people who merited respect and consideration. It was seeing him crouched down with them for the hose demonstration that really gave her ovaries a squeeze, his arms around a boy and girl as they helped steady the stream of water, laughing and grinning and clearly having the time of their lives.

She'd given up on the idea of a biological child of her own. But she'd been rethinking all kinds of things since her relationship with Caleb had changed. How could she see him like this and not imagine him with a child? The idea of it had been circling around her brain for a couple weeks now—that it wasn't outside the realm of possibility. Now it reached up and grabbed her by the throat.

She thought back to what he'd said on their run right before Fiona left for school. That he'd want kids with the right woman—if she wanted them. He'd made it crystal clear he thought she was the right woman. Not that he'd pressured her at all. She knew what it had to be costing him to let her set the pace, and she was grateful for his seemingly unending patience.

But...a baby.

Did she still want that? Did she even want to think about taking on that kind of commitment this late in life? She was thirty-six. Not ancient but definitely into that high-risk pregnancy age bracket. And if she had a baby now, she'd be—oh God—fifty-five by the time he or she left for college. But with Caleb it wouldn't be like it had been with Fi. She wouldn't be doing it alone.

And that was a whole lot of getting ahead of herself. There was a lot of distance between dating and sleeping together and marriage and babies.

But as she slid into her car to head back home, she glanced back at him, surrounded by preschoolers and thought, *Maybe.*

"CALEB, WE'RE HERE."

He opened his eyes, blinking at the three-story Victorian with the turret and a wrap-around porch. For a moment his brain swam in old grief, seeing a slightly more run-down version of the house on a cloudy day half a lifetime ago. The present snapped into focus as the last wisps of sleep cleared from his brain.

Home. He was home.

Scrubbing a hand over his face, he looked over at Emerson. "Sorry I passed out on you."

"After the night you had, you needed it. Feel a little better?"

A fully-involved warehouse fire had sucked up last night and stretched his shift by several hours, so they'd gotten a late start. His body ached from napping in the truck, and a low-grade headache gripped his skull. But that would fade as he got out, got moving. He'd certainly functioned through worse and on less sleep. "Yeah. Thanks for driving."

"It was no problem. It's a pretty drive."

The front door opened and a blonde woman stepped out onto the porch.

"That'll be the start of the welcoming committee. C'mon. You're about to have your brain explode with too many names to remember. Nobody will expect you to get them all on the first try." Caleb slid out of the passenger seat as the first of his sisters came down the steps.

"Caleb! You're finally here!" Kennedy leapt, and he caught her in a swinging hug.

"Good to be here. Great to see you." Setting her on her feet, he held her at arm's length. Contentment practically glowed out of every pore. "Marriage and mommyhood look good on you."

"I'll absolutely take that compliment. Caroline thinks sleep is for pussies." She linked her arm through his and turned to Emerson. "Now, introduce me."

"Kennedy, this is my girlfriend, Emerson Aldridge. Emerson, my sister Kennedy Kincaid."

Kennedy sighed. "That never gets old."

Caleb pointed to her. "Newlywed."

"Got it." Emerson smiled. "Nice to meet you."

"It is *definitely* nice to meet you. We were starting to think he'd made you up."

"Why would I make her up?"

Another voice called down from the steps. "Well, it took you four years to bring her home. What were we supposed to think?"

He turned and snagged his youngest sister in another hug. "Athena. You were supposed to think I was taking my time and being respectful."

She squeezed him tight. "There's being respectful and there's being a chicken shit."

Rolling his eyes, he tweaked her hair. "You sound like Kyle." Turning to Emerson, he opened his mouth to make introductions, but she was staring.

"You...you're Athena Reynolds. Chef Athena Reynolds."

Athena laughed. "Apparently my reputation precedes me."

Emerson fixed him with an accusatory stare. "How many *other* famous siblings do you have?"

"I'm not sure internet famous counts as famous," Athena qualified.

"Are you kidding? I freaking *love* The Misfit Kitchen! My daughter and I watch every week."

Athena jerked a thumb in Emerson's direction. "I like this one, Caleb. You did good. Now, come eat. Dinner waits for no man in my kitchen. You can unload later."

"Yes, ma'am." He held out a hand for Emerson's. Contentment slid through him as she twined her fingers with his and climbed the steps.

"We're being fed by Athena Reynolds!" she hissed.

"We always did have good eats around here."

Inside they were greeted by more of the family and put through the gauntlet of hugs and handshakes from his eldest sister, Pru; her husband, Flynn; their teenage daughter, Ari, and baby, Bailey; Kennedy's husband, Xander, with their infant daughter; Athena's husband, Logan; and the last of adopted Reynolds daughters, Maggie; her husband, Porter; and their brand-new baby girl, Faith. Caleb had to hand it to Emerson...she took the crazy in stride.

Xander bounced Caroline. "This one's fussy. I'm gonna see if I can get her to go down for a bit, so we can eat in peace."

As he strode out of the room, Porter pulled Caleb into a back-thumping hug. "It's good to see you, brother."

"Back, atcha, Papa."

Porter beamed, the picture of a proud daddy. Considering how long he'd waited for Maggie, Caleb wished him every shred of happiness.

"Everybody sit!" Athena ordered.

With the well-ordered chaos he remembered, everyone snagged a serving dish and carried it to the long farmhouse table. He had so many memories at this table, and he loved that the girls had kept it when they'd updated the house to an inn. Conversation flew fast as food was dished and passed. Beside him on the long bench, Emerson sat quiet. He couldn't quite tell if she was overwhelmed or just absorbing it all.

"Emerson, don't mind us," Pru told her. "We're a loud, noisy bunch. Just jump into the conversation."

"It's sink or swim around here," Xander confirmed, slipping onto the bench beside Kennedy.

She laughed. "I don't know how I'm going to remember everybody!"

"No, no, I've got you," Ari said. "You narrate romance, right?"

Emerson's lips twitched. "Yeah."

The teen moved slowly around the table, pointing. "Kennedy is married to Xander. He was her high school sweetheart before she moved abroad for a decade, and they were a second chance romance situation when Kennedy came home for Joan's funeral. They now have Caroline.

"Athena met Logan when she came in for Kennedy's wedding, but they didn't get together until after she left her fancy restaurant in Chicago on account of her business partner boyfriend was a cheating douchecanoe. Award-winning chef and organic farmer. I mean the foodie romance practically wrote itself.

"Maggie and Porter were foster sibs—I think at the same time you were here, Caleb." She looked at him to confirm.

"Yep. Same time."

"Right, so he was in love with her since basically forever, but they were just friends. Sad! And then Maggie totally fell out at work out in California because she'd been working herself too hard for, like, years, and had to take a forced break, so she came home and he *finally* did something about it. Now she's a recovering attorney and they have baby Faith.

"And *my* parents were maybe the best story of the bunch—not that I'm biased—"

"Oh, not at all," Pru agreed with a laugh.

"Well, we all know if you hadn't faked that whole engagement because of my social worker, you probably wouldn't have married Dad, you wouldn't have Bailey, and I'd be changing a lot fewer diapers."

"Fake engagement?" Emerson asked with interest.

"It's a long, complicated story," Flynn admitted.

"With a happy ending." Ari folded her hands under her chin and batted her eyes. "Me."

Caleb laughed. "Oh, Fiona would really like you."

"And Fiona is…?"

Emerson relaxed at the question. "My daughter. She's a few years older than you. A freshman at Belmont."

He could see Ari doing the math, wondering about the ages, but she didn't ask. Her own mother was young to have a teenager. Instead, she propped her chin in one hand. "Your turn! How did you two meet?"

The shift in energy was palpable in Emerson's sharp intake of breath. The kid had no way of knowing theirs wasn't a fun, romantic story.

Caleb reached for her hand and opened his mouth to say that they'd been friends for a long time, but Emerson spoke first.

"He saved me."

"Wait…what?"

She cut a glance toward him, squeezing his hand before continuing. "My daughter is actually my best friend's daughter. Several years ago, the two of them were in a car accident. Caleb was first on the scene and got Fiona out. Micah didn't make it." Sympathetic murmurs rose up around the table, but Caleb couldn't take his eyes off Emerson.

Her throat worked, and he knew she was fighting the emotion that always came up with the accident. "I met him when I came to the hospital for Fi." She lifted her gaze to his. "I was out of my mind with worry. Nobody would tell me anything, and there you were, like this island of calm. You took me back, told me about Micah and gave me time to fall apart before you took me to Fiona. Do you remember what you said to me?"

He'd said a lot that night, but he couldn't recall anything that hadn't been strictly professional.

"You said, 'Just keep breathing. I've got you.' I didn't think anything of it at the time. I was devastated and you were offering comfort. But you stuck around. In those days and weeks after, you kept coming by. I'd hit that point when I was on the verge of falling apart, when I'd think, there is no way I can do this, and there you'd be to do whatever I needed, *be* whatever I needed, convincing me that I could. Making sure that I just kept breathing. And I could because you were there."

Caleb's throat went thick with emotion. Yeah, he'd done all that. He'd wanted to lessen their pain however he could. But he'd never really known how much of an impact his efforts had made. "You—" He had to clear his throat. "You never said."

"Just because we never talked about it doesn't mean it didn't happen." Her mouth quirked in a half smile. "And, in my defense, you spend a lot of time seeming to read my mind, so I guess I thought you knew. You saved me every bit as much as you saved my daughter."

*Then let me watch out for you both for the rest of my life.*

"That's beautiful," Ari sighed.

Right. They had an audience. Caleb swallowed down everything he wanted to say. There'd be opportunity later. This wasn't the time or the place. But he couldn't hold back the quiet joy that seemed to pulse through him with every thump of his heart.

"All of y'all are setting the bar so incredibly high for my future relationships," the girl continued. He wasn't quite sure if it was a complaint or not.

"Hold out until you find it, kid." Emerson glanced back up at him and smiled with an answering joy. "It's absolutely worth the wait."

# CHAPTER 12

"Foster or significant other?"

It had become the official first question of everybody Emerson met at the reunion—and there were dozens of people here, way more than the inn itself could house. She'd long since lost track of all the people she'd met and the stories she'd heard, but she'd fallen into a rhythm.

"Significant other." She pointed across the yard to where Caleb had been pulled into conversation with Wyatt Sullivan. "Foster."

The blonde brightened. "Oh! You're Caleb's. Nice to meet you. I'm Abbey Whittaker. Neither foster nor significant other, but long-time friend of the family."

Emerson looked around at all the families, young and older. "There are so many. I had no idea. I kinda feel like we should have nametags with dates on them for the ones who were Joan's."

"Like a class reunion. That's a great idea. I'll suggest it to Pru for next year."

"It's a testament to who Joan was that they've all come back. That they're so happy and well-adjusted, considering how many came from such sad beginnings. I wish I could've met her."

"She was a force of nature. When she died, things were…pretty rocky among her daughters. I wasn't sure what would happen. But they came together, stronger than ever, and made all this." Abbey gestured at the inn and spa and the outbuilding that housed Athena's Misfit Kitchen, where she periodically hosted cooking classes on top of filming her hit web TV cooking series.

"I think it's even more amazing that they've managed to maintain the family ties she established with all the others." She'd seen first-hand that actual family ties could be brittle.

Pru sank down into an empty chair, Bailey on her lap. "It's work but definitely worth it. Even if hanging out around here it's often like our own version of *Cheaper By The Dozen*."

"Is that as awesome as I imagine it to be?" Emerson asked.

"Mmm, it can be a mixed bag. But for most of us, we came from lousy families of origin, so being brought into a family where we could count on others was something we learned to appreciate and protect. Caleb was unusual. He had a great relationship with his parents before they died. Mom would have adopted him, but he wanted to stay a Romero, which is entirely understandable."

"He definitely seems to have glommed on to the sibling thing, though. He and Kyle are tight."

Abbey stiffened, sucking in a hard breath through her nose.

Emerson went brows up. "Ah, let me guess. You're the one he messed things up with."

"What do you know about it?" Her tone was more alarmed than accusatory.

*Definitely a story there.* "Not a thing except that Kyle knows he screwed up and doesn't think it can be fixed."

"Then he's smarter than he looks." Abbey shoved up from the chair. "I need a drink. Does anybody else want something?"

When she and Pru declined, Abbey stalked away.

"Sorry. I didn't mean to step in it."

"Kyle's her trigger point. Always has been. There's a lot of hurt there."

"It's none of my business, but I admit to being super curious about what happened."

"You and me both. She's never said specifically. Shuts it down if anybody brings it up, as you saw. We gave up asking about it years ago."

Bailey squirmed in Pru's lap and reached toward Emerson. Her heart gave a little bump. "May I?"

"Oh, of course."

Pru handed over her daughter. Bailey pressed both pudgy hands to Emerson's cheeks and stared into her with big, blue eyes. "Kiss."

"Oh, well okay then." She accepted a sticky baby kiss. It shouldn't have been charming, but it was. As Bailey wound both arms around her neck, Emerson cuddled her close, relishing the feel of the tiny, warm body against hers and the scent of baby shampoo and cookies. "I skipped this stage since mine was fourteen when I got her. I didn't think I'd miss it." But there was a little ache under her breastbone at the idea of never doing this, never having this herself.

"It's a big change taking on a teenager when you didn't expect it. Mom was in the process of adopting Ari when she died, so I ended up shifting mental gears from sister to mom. It was tough, but I at least knew what I was getting into. I chose it. Yours was harder. I'm so sorry about your friend."

Emerson inclined her head, acknowledging the condolence. "Fiona changed everything. All the things I wanted, all the things I thought were important, shifted that night. Everything the last four years has centered around her. It had to. She was so broken after the accident. Nothing else mattered but getting her through that. Now she's in college, and she's happy and well-adjusted, and I know a big part of that is because of Caleb. Because he cut open a vein and bled for her in sharing his experience with losing his parents."

"Has he ever talked about it with you?"

"No, and that's fine. That's their shared pain point. I don't need to know to be grateful. He's been an amazing friend to me."

"And now he's something more."

Emerson began rubbing absent circles on Bailey's back. "I didn't expect this. I had no idea he felt more for me than friendship. I'm still kind of adjusting to it."

"I think I understood better than everyone else why Caleb waited to say anything. It's hard to balance motherhood and womanhood."

"*Yes.*" It was a relief to hear someone else say it. "I hadn't even looked at him like that before." At Pru's raised eyebrow, she offered a rueful smile. "Okay, maybe I looked, but I certainly didn't have any expectations. Not with him being so much younger than me."

Pru scanned the yard in that automatic way Emerson had come to realize meant she was checking on guests. "I met Flynn when he flew in right before Kennedy's wedding. We'd just made the decision that I'd be the one to adopt Ari, and I knew my life was going to irrevocably change. I was going to be a mom. In the beginning, even though I chose it willingly, I felt a little like a cage door was shutting on me, and I decided I was going to take one thing for myself before it did. So I propositioned him."

Emerson choked a little. "Seriously?"

Pru shrugged. "I figured at least I'd have the memories of a blistering affair with a gorgeous Irishman to keep me warm at night. As fate would have it, I kept the Irishman when he fell in love with us both."

"And now you have this little one." Bailey's head had grown heavy on her shoulder as she slid into sleep.

Pru beamed, the picture of motherly bliss. "We do. We're an unconventional family, but we work."

"Is it weird? Having two kids with such a big age gap?"

"Yes and no. Ari was so hungry for family, she was ecstatic when I turned up pregnant. She's been such a big help with all the babies. It's a little strange thinking about the fact that she'll likely be out on her own and maybe married herself before Bailey's out of high school." She cut a glance in Emerson's direction. "But that's not what you're asking, is it?"

"I don't guess it is. I'm older than you by several years. Nearly a decade older than Caleb. I gave up on the idea of having children years ago. I'm at the other end of the spectrum. That cage door is open now—God, I feel like such a terrible person even saying that. Fiona wasn't a prison."

"Not terrible. Human," Pru corrected. "Kids under the best of circumstances can be a lot. Traumatized kids are a whole other level. There's no shame in feeling some relief that a bit of that burden is lifted."

Hearing another woman, another mother, say that was something of a benediction.

"Anyway, I find myself thinking about kids—the idea of my actual, biological children—wondering if it's something I gave up because I didn't think I could rather than because I had to. And if it is something I want, there's this ticking clock in the back of my brain telling me I don't have that much time left. Which is a crappy place to be because having a child isn't a decision that can or should be made fast. It's a big shift in my thinking, and I don't quite know what to do with it."

"What made you give up on the idea before?"

"I was alone and on the heels of a breakup with a long-time boyfriend who ended up cheating on me. There is no amount of money on earth that would induce me to be a single parent again."

"It's definitely different doing it alone. I was lucky enough never to have to do that. I always had my sisters, and then Flynn. But you have Caleb."

Emerson sighed. "Yeah. Yeah, I do, and he makes it really easy to imagine what could be. But it's way too soon to know anything about the future."

"From what it sounded like last night, the feelings have been there for both of you for years. It's just the acting on them that's relatively new."

Was that true? Had she, on some level, been sliding in deeper with him all this time, even without the expectation of reciprocity? "Maybe."

"It seems to me like you're looking for some kind of certainty. And I hate to break it to you, but that doesn't exist. You know what kind of man he is. That's the most certainty you're going to get. Everything else is a leap of faith. If you think you might want kids with Caleb, talk to him. Figure out where he stands and whether that's something you'd be on the same page about."

Emerson gave her a sidelong glance. "Bring up kids after dating for six weeks?"

Pru laughed. "Talking about the possibility doesn't mean do it tomorrow. And if it's something you do want and he doesn't, then it'd be better to know that now than later."

She met his gaze from across the yard and thought back to their quiet morning a few weeks before.

*I want it all, Em.*

Did he really mean everything? And if he did, was she prepared to take that leap?

CALEB WATCHED Emerson where she sat on the porch with the baby drowsing against her shoulder. Her posture was relaxed, curled around Bailey with the kind of affection that spoke of legitimately loving children. Something about the picture they made reached up to grab him by the heart and twist. She should have the chance to be a mother on her terms. He wanted to give that to her, along with every other dream she'd put on hold.

Porter joined him, following his line of sight. "It's a powerful thing, seeing the woman you love with a baby."

*The woman you love.* He waited for the jolt at that, but none came. And why should it? Maybe he hadn't named it, but he'd been in love with Emerson for a long, long time. If anyone could understand that, it would be Porter. "Is that how it is with Maggie and Faith?"

"Yeah. Faith is our miracle. But, actually, I meant before. Seeing her with Bailey the day she was born is what finally made me speak up about my feelings for her."

That surprised Caleb enough to pull his attention. "Really? Why?"

"Because I wanted that with her, and if she didn't or couldn't feel the same, then I needed to get to work getting over it."

Everything in Caleb rebelled at the thought. No, he'd waited for Emerson for years. No way was he giving her up. She was enough, all on her own. But as he glanced back to see her pressing a kiss to Bailey's curls, he got that twist in his heart again.

"I thought I was okay without it. Kids were just this kind of hypothetical thing I could take or leave. Then I look at her like that and...damn. I feel all this possessive, primal shit. Obviously, I'm more than the sum of my hormones, but what if it matters more to me than I realized?"

"So you have an honest conversation about it."

From the porch, Emerson met his gaze, her expression serious before her lips curved into a half smile.

Could they really have that conversation? They'd circled around it as she'd had those epiphanies about her age and how what she'd wanted wasn't out of reach after all. She hadn't come outright and said she still wanted it. More to the point, she hadn't said she wanted it with him. But it felt like they'd turned some kind of corner in their relationship this weekend. As if maybe it had finally become real to her as a relationship, not just as some kind of a fling.

"I don't want to pressure her. This between us is all new for her, and she just got Fi out of the house."

"You know her. I figure you're capable of finding a way to discuss it without being all, 'I want you to have my babies.'"

Fuck, why did the idea of that make his dick twitch? "I just don't know that she's at a place where I can ask that yet."

"Wouldn't it be better to know before you get in any deeper with her?"

"I don't know if I can get in any deeper."

Porter laughed and clapped him on the shoulder. "Brother, there's always deeper with the one you love."

Well, wasn't that both wonderful and terrifying?

Abbey Whittaker sidled up. "Hello, boys."

"Hey! I wondered whether I'd get to see you this trip." Caleb pulled her in for a hug.

She looked good, her blonde hair loose around her shoulders, her ready smile in place. But the longer he studied her face, the more he could tell that something was off.

"I met your girl. I like her."

"I'm pretty keen on her myself. How's life treating you back in The Ridge?"

"Can't complain. I've been working at the spa since it opened. Business is booming."

He was trying to work out whether he could or should ask her if something was wrong in front of Porter, when she linked her arm through his.

"Can I talk to you? In private?"

"Sure."

Porter gave a two-fingered wave. "I'm off to find my wife. See y'all later."

Caleb followed her through the crowd, noting the tension in her shoulders. Something was definitely wrong. They circled around to the front door of the spa. It was closed for the reunion this weekend, so nobody was inside. The interior was dark and cool, but for the light streaming through the skylights in the atrium of the lobby. The faint burble of water from a small water feature was the only sound other than their footsteps.

"What's up, Abs? You seem a little tense."

The smile was gone when she rounded on him. "I need to ask you something, and I need you to be honest with me."

"Okay."

"What has Kyle said about me?"

He'd suspected it might be something to do with Kyle, but he hadn't expected this. "In what context? That's pretty broad."

She crossed her arms in a self-protective gesture. "Emerson said something about me being the one Kyle screwed up with. I want to know what he said."

Was she agitated at what Kyle might have said or that Caleb himself might know something? "I'm the one who said that. Because he did."

The knuckles of the fingers gripping her elbows went white. "What did he tell you?"

"Nothing. He's never told me what went down all those years ago. But you don't suddenly stay away from one of your closest friends unless something major happened." Caleb had his suspicions about the nature of that something major, given how things had been changing between Kyle and Abbey that last summer. But if they'd crossed that line from friends to something more, he'd never had it confirmed. "All he's ever said when I asked was that it was his fault and to leave it alone."

She released a slow breath, the tension going out of her shoulders. "At least he can be honest about something."

"What wasn't he honest about?"

Abbey shook her head. "Doesn't matter."

"If it doesn't matter, why are you still upset about it?"

Her eyes flashed with a mix of temper and hurt. "I didn't say I was upset."

Caleb folded his arms. "You dragged me off away from everybody to ask me about something that happened more than ten years ago. If you weren't upset, you would have let it go."

"I just wanted to know how he was spinning the narrative and why he was talking about something from back then."

"He's not spinning anything. The only narrative he's ever put forward is that what happened was his fault and an apology can't fix it."

Abbey looked off toward the big picture window that opened onto the mountains. "Maybe it might have back then. But after all this time..." She trailed off on a heavy sigh.

"Why won't you two just talk to each other?"

Her shoulders tensed back up. "I don't want to talk to Kyle."

"Look, you don't have to be friends. Maybe you can't go back to what you were before after all this time." Which was a damned shame because they were perfect for each other. "But for God's sake, you both need closure. The pair of you need to put on your grown-up pants and have the shitty, awkward conversation you've been avoiding all this time so you can both move on with your lives. Life is too fucking short to be carrying around all these regrets."

"I don't have regrets. There's no point in them. You can't go back to change the past."

"But if you both pull your heads out of your asses, you can have the future."

Abbey's lips curved into a sad smile. "I'm happy for you about Emerson, Caleb. But don't go putting your love goggles on everybody. We don't all get happy endings." Without another word, she left him standing there in the dark atrium.

Stubborn as mules. Both of them. They were too mired in the past, in their respective hurts, to try to fix things. But this was as close as he'd gotten to confirmation that something *had* happened between them that went beyond the friends they'd always been. How could they let one tough conversation stand between them and what they both clearly wanted?

How could he? He wanted a life with Emerson. Marriage, children, the whole shebang. He was willing to wait for them until she was ready, but Porter was right. He needed to know whether they were on the same page or not. And if not...he had to figure out whether that was something he could live with.

# CHAPTER 13

*C*aleb stayed quiet on the drive home. Not broody, but obviously thinking hard about something. Emerson might have been anxious about that but for the fact that he kept her hand in his for as much of the trip as he could. She'd been doing a lot of thinking herself about her conversation with Pru. Being around all those families, especially Caleb's sisters, with all their newlywed and new parent vibes, had her biological clock sounding a gong.

Maybe that should've been scary. Instead, the possibilities excited and energized her. She was starting to see how things could be with Caleb. That wasn't a clarity she'd ever had in prior relationships. Was it because she knew herself and what she wanted better than she did before? Maybe. But as he pulled into his driveway, she looked over at him, taking in his profile and the shape of the jaw she now knew by touch. She could see the possibilities because she knew him. Because she loved him.

The realization slammed into her.

*Holy shit.*

Shutting off the truck, he glanced her way. "You okay?"

For a moment she couldn't speak.

She loved Caleb. She was *in love* with him.

Because she didn't want to just blurt that out until she'd had more time to turn it over in her brain, she scrambled for something else to say. "I like your family."

His smile lit up his face. "They really liked you."

Because she couldn't just sit there and didn't know what else to say, she slid out of the truck. They grabbed their bags and headed toward her house. It wasn't a question that he'd be staying the night, since he'd be on shift again tomorrow morning. So many things between them had simply been implied. They fit on multiple levels, and suddenly, she didn't want to leave things implied. She wanted to talk about the future and what they both wanted.

As they stepped into her front entryway, she turned. "Caleb, I wanted to ask you something."

He dropped his bag. "Me too." Sliding her duffel bag off her shoulder, he backed her against the wall. "Yes."

The possessive move already had her blood going hot, her mind not quite able to hang on to the threads of conversation. "What?"

"Whatever it is the answer is yes."

He couldn't just say that. "You don't know what I'm going to ask."

"It's you. I know you, so I have a good idea. And I'm all in."

Caging her in, he took her mouth in a deep, devouring kiss that fogged her brain and set her on fire. Rising to her toes, she pressed against him. Serious conversation could wait until later. It might even be better had naked. That was logical, right?

The light in the living room clicked on. "What the actual hell?"

Caleb's embrace was the only thing stopping Emerson from jerking away from him like a guilty teenager at the sound of her own teenager's voice.

Shock, guilt, and dread swirled through her in a noxious cocktail of emotion. Emerson didn't know how to react. They were certainly busted.

"What are you doing home?" Okay, probably not the best thing to lead with, but it was all she could come up with.

"Do I need to announce when I come home now? I guess maybe I do."

Heat burned her cheeks. Thank God they hadn't gotten any further in the naked portion of the program. "That's not...this is... Caleb and I are..."

Fi crossed her arms. "Sleeping together, obviously."

"We are in a relationship." Caleb's tone was even, but it held a faint warning.

It was nice to know one of them could be calm.

"A going away for the weekend together kind of relationship. Where's Mooch?"

"With Paisley." As Emerson searched her daughter's face, she recognized the strain and signs of tears. This wasn't just upset and shock over her and Caleb. "Honey, why did you come home? What's wrong?"

"Why does something have to be wrong? Maybe I just wanted to see you. I had no idea you'd leave town without even telling me."

The guilt dug deep between her ribs. She'd considered mentioning it but hadn't wanted to get into...well, all of this before the trip. Fiona had been busy with school and seemed content and settled. Emerson hadn't wanted to rock the boat. And a part of her had just wanted to do something for just herself, without consideration of her duties as a mother.

"I wasn't deliberately keeping you in the dark."

Fiona shot her an *Oh please* look, and Emerson realized she'd blown this. She should have made the time sooner and dealt with the hard conversation.

Resigned to facing it now, she struggled to put herself back firmly in the role of parent. "I'm sorry I wasn't here for you. I didn't know you needed me. You didn't call."

"I figured I'd just wait for you."

Did she mean hours or all weekend? "How long have you been here?"

"It doesn't matter. Long enough. They said at the station that Caleb was out of town and that you'd gone with him."

She'd found out about them from the fire station. Emerson knew how much they liked to razz Caleb about her. There was no telling what they'd said to Fiona under the assumption that she'd already known. Shit. This wasn't going to be an easy fix.

Turning to Caleb, she kept her voice low. "I think I need to handle this on my own."

His face clouded. She knew he felt like she was shutting him out. And maybe she was, a little. But it had been just her and Fiona for a long time, and this conversation was for them and them alone.

Before he could press the issue, she continued. "It was my bad decision that got us here. No reason for it to spill over on you. I'll touch base in a little while."

With a reluctant nod, he released her. "You know where to find me."

Emerson stayed where she was until he shut the door quietly behind him. Fiona still stood in the living room, arms crossed, a belligerent set to her jaw. There was hurt beneath the anger. Emerson would have to dig her way through one to deal with the other.

Bracing herself, she crossed to one of the chairs and sat. "I can tell you're upset. I know this must have been a shock."

"You think?"

Under the circumstances, she let the bitter sarcasm pass. "The truth is, I didn't know how to tell you."

"Really? That's what you're going with? How hard is it to say, 'Oh hey Fi, Caleb and I are dating'?"

Because Emerson would have placed money on that simple declaration going over like a lead balloon. "I know you have a special relationship with him. I wasn't sure how you'd feel about it."

Fiona flung herself onto the sofa. "So why didn't you ask me?"

Lacing her hands, Emerson searched for the words. "That's a fair question. I don't have a good answer. I guess I was afraid."

"Of what?"

"That it would change things between you and Caleb. Between you and me. That I'd take the risk to be with him and it wouldn't work out and every major relationship in my life would be damaged because of it." Hell, she was still afraid of that.

"It didn't sound like it was in danger of not working out."

A fact which Emerson was putting a pin in for later because she still wanted to talk to him about their future. But she wouldn't discuss that with Fiona. "It's early still. Either way, I'm sorry my cowardice hurt you."

Instead of acknowledging the apology, Fi slouched into the sofa. "Are you in love with him?"

*Yes.* But she didn't feel right sharing that with her daughter before telling Caleb himself. "I feel very strongly for him. This relationship isn't casual." It was maybe the very antithesis of casual, if their conversation went the way she hoped.

"Whose idea was it?"

Emerson wasn't sure why that mattered, but clearly it did. "His. He's had feelings for me for a long time."

Her nostrils flared. "How long have y'all been sneaking around?"

Temper snuck through the hard-won patience. "We are grown adults. We're not sneaking anywhere. But to answer the question I think you're getting at, we didn't get involved romantically until after you left for school."

"Because I was finally out of the way."

Horrified at the resignation in her daughter's voice—and at the barest hint of truth to it—Emerson shook her head. "No. Because he didn't want to do anything to distract me from giving you everything you needed."

Fiona snorted out a humorless laugh and seemed to switch gears. "I can't believe you left this weekend."

She said it as if that was significant. Emerson scrambled to figure out what she'd missed. "Do you want to talk about why you came home?"

Fiona's lip trembled, her eyes welling before temper rose again to block it out. "If you don't know already, I'm not going to tell you."

It had been a long time since she'd seen this moody, passive-aggressive attitude. "Fi."

Fiona shoved up from the sofa, and stalked away. "I'm going back to school."

"Fiona, please—"

The slam of the door was her only answer.

* * *

CALEB PACED HIS HOUSE, stalking circles through the living room and kitchen and back again. Irritation clenched his shoulders. He hated being shut out. And it irritated him that he was irritated. Fiona wasn't his kid. He objectively understood why Emerson wanted to talk to her alone. But he didn't like the two of them presenting anything but a united front.

He grabbed a beer from the fridge, twisting the top off with more force than strictly necessary. Taking a sip, he exhaled a slow breath. Okay, at least seventy-five percent of his annoyance was that they'd been interrupted. Not just the impending naked time —although, definitely that—but the serious relationship discussion he recognized they both wanted to have. They'd both been thinking about it the whole drive back from Eden's Ridge. He hadn't needed her to say a word to confirm that. They were going to level up, get more serious. Or he was pretty damned sure that was where they'd been headed. Was this thing with Fiona going to derail that? That was his big fear. That all the progress Emerson had made the past couple of months would be, yet again, overshadowed by her role as mom.

The back door opened. Caleb set the beer aside as Emerson came in.

"That was fast. How did it go?" But he could already tell from the lines of strain around her mouth.

She sighed and swiped up his beer for a long pull herself. "Not great. She stormed out and went back to school."

Caleb winced. "That bad? What did she say?"

Emerson set the bottle down and sagged against the counter. "There was a lot of angry sarcasm. And she was especially upset about this weekend for reasons I can't figure out. I must have missed something, but damned if I can think what."

Knowing she would beat herself up about that, he pulled her in. "She'll calm down and come around. She just has to get used to things."

Burrowing against him, she pressed her cheek to his chest. "You were right. I should have told her sooner."

"Why didn't you?" At her slight stiffening, he added, "That's not a criticism. I really want to know."

"At first because I didn't know how. And then because I didn't think we'd possibly last, and I just... The past couple of months with you have been a fantasy. I didn't want the bubble to pop."

It had well and truly burst now. But he didn't miss what she'd said. That she hadn't thought they'd last. That implied she thought differently now.

Tipping her face up to look into those big blue eyes, he stroked her cheek. "We can survive real life, Emerson." He needed her to believe that because he was willing to do whatever it took.

"Yes, I think we can. Which is part of what I wanted to talk to you about before teenagergeddon back there."

"Real life?" Were they about to really, truly start theirs?

"And the future. What we want ours to look like. You said you're all in. I want to know what that means."

She wanted a future with him. Caleb's heart tripped into a gallop. This conversation might just be the most important one of his life. "It means I'm in for anything you want." He wanted everything with this woman, but he thought saying so just now might be pushing too far, too fast.

Emerson studied him for several long moments before she seemed to steel herself. "What if I want a baby?"

Short of dropping down on one knee herself, she couldn't have surprised him more. He'd been so worried about pushing her too far, too fast, and here she was asking him for the thing he wanted most—the chance to make a literal life with her. A life that merged the best of both of them. His cock stiffened and reported for immediate duty.

"Yes."

Her head jerked back in shock. "What do you mean, 'yes'? You can't just say yes."

"Pardon me. I misspoke. Hell yes." He pulled her tighter against him so she could feel his body's enthusiastic support of that plan.

A tinge of something that was equal parts exasperation and fluster crept into her tone. "Think about what you're agreeing to. A baby means long-term commitment. Emotional. Financial. And the prospect of him or her eventually turning into that." She waved a hand in the general direction of her house, obviously encompassing Fiona's less than optimal reaction.

He couldn't stop the twitch of his lips. "Who are you trying to talk out of it here?"

"I'm just trying to be rational and realistic. It's only been a matter of weeks. It isn't a decision to make fast or lightly."

Of all the things he'd reassured her about, this would be the easiest. He framed her face between his palms. "I'll give you some rational realism: It's been four years, and I don't make this decision lightly. I love you. I want a life with you. And I'd love nothing more than to make a baby with you."

Her eyes swirled with emotion. "Caleb."

Catching the tear that managed to escape with his thumb, he searched her face. "Is that what you want?"

Her throat worked, and when she spoke, her voice was barely above a whisper. But he heard the answer he'd been waiting for. "Yes."

He couldn't stop the delighted grin from taking over his face. "Then let's make a baby." Reaching around to her back pocket, he slipped the phone out of it, deliberately engaging silent mode before laying it on the kitchen island.

"What? Now?"

Running his hands over her ass, down her thighs, he picked her up. "No time like the present."

Laughing, she wrapped her legs around him as he headed for his bedroom. "And here Pru said having the discussion didn't mean doing it tomorrow. It's literally tomorrow."

"You talked to Pru about this?"

"I wanted her perspective as the mom of a teenager and a toddler. She made me feel like it was possible."

God bless his sister. "Remind me to send her flowers later. Meanwhile, I intend to devote all my considerable stamina to making our tomorrow today."

"I still have my IUD."

"So we can practice. Lots and lots until you're ready to go for the real thing. The fact is, I want you. I always want you. And I want to make love to you in every conceivable way, in my bed, while I think about burying myself deep and spilling into you."

Emerson shivered. "Why is that so hot?"

"Biological imperative?"

As he turned into the hall, he heard the buzz of Emerson's phone vibrating on the counter. He paused as she glanced toward the kitchen. The last thing he wanted was to stop right now, but it was her call.

She looked back at him. "I want you to make love to me, in your bed, while we both think about you filling me up."

Her words made him shudder. But more than that, she was choosing to put them first. After all this time, all his patience, that was such a gift. He knew that wouldn't—couldn't—always be the case. But for tonight, she was his to love and cherish.

Taking her mouth with his, he turned into his room and tumbled them both onto the bed.

* * *

LETTING that call go to voicemail—whoever it was—felt monumental. Tonight, *finally*, she was putting herself and her needs first. That they totally coincided with Caleb's was a happy bonus.

He loved her. He wanted a life with her. The very idea of it was a miracle and filled her with so much joy she thought she'd burst. As he stripped her naked, the joy turned to desire, stark and ravenous. He made her *feel* everything as he worshipped her body, suckling her breasts and then moving lower, until she was wet and writhing and desperate.

She flexed her fingers in his hair, tugging. "Caleb, please. I need you."

Lifting his head, he met her gaze, his own full of volcanic heat as he crawled up her body and settled between her thighs.

"Love you." He took her mouth in a claiming kiss, and she tasted her pleasure on his tongue. "Love you so fucking much."

Then he slid into her, slow and deep and perfect, filling up all the empty places inside her with every slow, deliberate stroke. Caleb Romero was her match, in every way. She wished there was no IUD because she loved the idea of his hard, hot length bare and buried deep inside her, spilling into her when her own release pulled him over. She loved the idea of conceiving here, tonight, as a sign of their commitment. Of their forever. The thought of it had her orgasm ripping up from her toes, her whole body clenching around him in a brutal, glorious grip. And then Caleb was coming and coming, emptying everything he was inside her before collapsing.

Emerson was grateful for his forethought to brace himself on his forearms so he didn't completely crush her because she didn't have the energy or will to move. For long minutes, they could only gasp, their frantic hearts slowing as sweat-slicked skin began to cool.

When she thought she could speak, she croaked, "I should probably wait to have my IUD removed."

"Second thoughts already?"

"No, but that was the best sex of my life and I'd like to have as much of it as possible."

The rumble of his laugh vibrated her chest and she felt him already stirring inside her as he took her mouth in a kiss. Hell yes, she could go for another round of that.

From somewhere on the floor, his phone began to ring.

Caleb hesitated. "It might be work."

She slapped his bare ass. "Go ahead. I'm not going anywhere."

He rolled off her, and she instantly regretted the loss of his warmth. Another two rings completed by the time he dug the phone out of his pants from the pile of clothes they'd discarded.

"Hello?"

The good humor on his face melted in an instant. "What?"

As the person on the other end continued to speak, he glanced at her, his expression shifting to a neutral mask. Feeling suddenly cold, she pulled the sheet up over her breasts.

"Where?" Another pause. "Yeah, we're on the way."

A huge, encompassing dread draped over Emerson like a lead cloak as he hung up the phone. That carefully neutral face terrified her. She'd seen that face before, on a rainy night over four years ago.

Caleb sat on the bed and took her hand. She wanted to pull away, wanted to stop whatever was about to come out of his mouth. She wanted to rewind to ten minutes ago, when life was full of possibilities and promise. Because she understood that whatever he said would be yet another dividing line.

"There's been an accident."

## CHAPTER 14

"*I* came as soon as I could. What's going on?" Paisley demanded.

Caleb scrubbed a hand down his face. "Fiona's in surgery."

"Oh my God." Her gaze strayed to Emerson, who sat across the waiting room, arms wrapped around herself, rocking in one of the molded plastic chairs. "What happened?"

"Fi found out about us tonight. It didn't go well, and she left upset. Emerson missed her call to apologize, and the voicemail she left cut off when she got T-boned." He'd worked more accident scenes than he could count, had seen more than one as they happened—including the one that had taken Micah's life. But nothing had ever shaken him the way hearing Fiona's voice cut off with a crash and the sound of shattering glass. Nothing except the absolute anguish on Emerson's face as she heard it too. "I had to take Emerson's phone away so she wouldn't keep torturing herself with the voicemail."

Paisley covered her mouth. "What have the doctors said?"

"Not a helluva lot. She was already in surgery when we got here. But Em's bad. I know she's scared out of her mind. This is literally her worst nightmare come true and she's totally shut down and shut me out. I know she's finding some way to blame herself for this, and I can't get through to her. I was hoping you'd have better luck."

Calling Paisley was the only thing he could think to do. There was nothing he could fix, no way to make it better. If anything happened to Fiona, it would devastate Emerson in a way she'd never recover from.

Paisley squeezed his arm. "I'll try to talk to her."

He watched her take a seat by Emerson, pulling her into a hug. That should have been him comforting her. Should have been him she could lean on. But from the moment he'd taken her hand to give her the news, she'd been pulling away, deep into herself. Blaming herself and, given the new distance between them, probably him, too. But he didn't know for sure because she was barely speaking.

He couldn't stand this. He had to find something to *do*. Some way to make this better. Maybe he could use some of his contacts to find out…something. He had to know somebody working on shift right now. Surely they could give a status update or an estimate for how much longer the surgery should last.

But before he could try to find someone, a doctor came into the waiting room. "Fiona Gaffney?"

Emerson bolted to her feet and swayed. Paisley wrapped an arm around her waist, stabilizing her. Caleb braced himself.

"I'm Dr. Norris, the surgeon who operated on Fiona. And you're her…?"

"Mother. Guardian. It's complicated. Is she…?"

"She came through surgery just fine and should make a full recovery."

Emerson clutched Paisley and just closed her eyes for a moment, murmuring his own sentiment. "Thank God."

Profound relief nearly took Caleb out at the knees. Fiona was okay. Emerson would be okay. Everything else was just details. They'd figure it out. He was good at the details.

Caleb listened as the doctor went over the specifics of Fiona's condition. With his EMT training, he understood more of the medical jargon, and he honestly wasn't sure how much of it Emerson was absorbing. He wanted to be able to tell her later if she needed it. Bruised ribs, some cuts, a torn rotator cuff, but it was the internal bleeding they'd repaired that had been the worst of it. She'd been lucky.

"When can I see her?" Emerson demanded.

"She's being moved to a room on the fourth floor. She'll be waking up soon. We want to keep her for a couple of days for observation, but there's no reason you can't see her."

"Can I stay with her?"

"Of course." Dr. Norris shook Emerson's hand. "The nurses will see that you get a blanket and pillow."

She blinked back the tears. "Thank you."

Even as the doctor walked away, Caleb was already making plans, sorting out the best way to make sure everything was covered so she wouldn't have to worry about anything but being there for Fiona.

Paisley was on it, too. "I'll run to the house and pack you a bag for the night. And don't you worry about Mooch. He's fine at my place hanging with Duke. They're having a little pupper bromance." She squeezed Emerson tight. "I'll be back as fast as I can."

Before she left, she met Caleb's gaze, clearly saying, *I'm leaving her with you. Take care of her.*

He nodded. Now that the uncertainty was past, maybe she'd start unbending a little.

As Paisley disappeared down the hall, he pulled out his phone. "I'll call in to give the guys the update and make arrangements for someone to cover my shift."

"That's not necessary." Emerson's voice was flat, toneless, and he recognized the armor going on as she prepared to see Fiona.

"Of course it is." Didn't she understand he was here for her?

"No."

She was still reacting, still operating as if she was on her own, as she had been four years ago. But this wasn't four years ago. This was now. She had him. "You're not dealing with this by yourself."

Emerson crossed her arms, as if she'd fly apart any moment. "I can't do this."

The gesture made him ache. Unable to stand it anymore, he reached for her, curling his hands around her stiff shoulders. "I have your back. I'll take care of whatever you need me to. You just need to keep breathing."

The eyes she lifted to his were shattered. "No, I can't do this with you."

"Do what?" What was this jittery, uncertain feeling clawing at his ribs? It crawled through him, growing bigger and fiercer with every word she spoke.

"Any of it. This was my fault. I should never have pursued things with you."

Panic. This was panic. He couldn't afford to give in to it. "I know you're upset. This whole thing has been terrifying, but it's not your fault."

Temper broke through the shield, and her voice shook. "She was driving upset because of me. She could have *died*, and I thought it was more important to be in your bed. I won't put anyone or anything else ahead of her ever again. I'm done, Caleb. We're done."

The words struck him like bullets, one after another. His breath wheezed out and he almost looked down at his own chest to check for a wound as the pain spread through him like poison. He hadn't heard her right. She was distraught and not thinking straight. "You don't mean that."

Her lips pressed into a thin line. "You know me better than almost anyone. Do I look anything other than serious?"

Her beautiful, beloved face was drawn with exhaustion. Every line of her body shouted resignation, and he had no doubt she was drowning in guilt and going down for the third time. Everything in him wanted to leap in and save her. It was what he did.

But he couldn't fight this. Not in this moment. And that absolutely killed him.

"I don't want to leave you alone." And maybe that was as much about him as her.

"I won't be. Paisley will be back soon. Go home, Caleb."

She needed him to walk away right now. As punishment? Penance? He didn't know. But he didn't know what else to do.

"Miss Aldridge?" A nurse approached. "I'm here to take you to your daughter."

Caleb released her and stepped back. His hands curled and uncurled, wanting to pull her in again and knowing he had to respect her wishes. For now. He handed over the phone he'd pocketed earlier. "Keep me updated on how she is. Please."

Emerson nodded and followed the nurse down the hall. No hesitation. No backward glance.

He'd keep the channels of communication open. She'd change her mind when she got past the scare. She had to. Because he didn't know how to live a life that wasn't centered around her and he didn't want to have to learn.

EMERSON SAT by Fiona's bedside, clutching her hand in both of hers, waiting for her girl to wake up. Even looking at her hurt, as if Emerson could feel every bruise, every cut, every torn muscle. But the truth was, she had hurt before she'd laid eyes on her daughter. Since the moment Caleb had taken her hand and said those dreaded words—again—and fear had cracked her in half. Every inch of her was raw, every nerve ending exposed. And all she wanted in the world was for the man she'd sent away to be here beside her.

She'd hurt him. He hadn't deserved that. But she knew him well enough to understand that nothing else would've gotten him to go. And he had to go. She couldn't be what Fiona needed and keep Caleb in her life. There just wasn't enough of her to go around, and Fi had to come first. Emerson owed her that.

And better she break things off with him now than later. Before she lost her mind and had a baby with him. How could she even think of bringing another child into the world, when she'd fucked up so badly with this one? It was just part of the long, lovely dream she'd been living in the past two months. One she'd let herself get entirely too immersed in.

Well, she was brutally awake now, slapped back to reality and her proper place. And if she wept for the loss of the dream, she couldn't apologize for it. She'd indulge the tears for a little while. Then she'd do what needed to be done, as she always had. But that would be for later, in the shower, where Fiona wouldn't hear. She'd gotten very good at hiding her grief over the years. At faking strength until she actually began to feel it.

Fiona's hand flexed in hers. "Auntie Em?"

At the faint rasp of her voice, Emerson straightened, clutching tighter at the hand she held. "I'm here, baby."

"Where am I?"

"In the hospital. You're gonna be okay." She sent up another silent prayer for the surgical team that had made that the truth.

"What happened?"

Emerson thought of the voicemail she'd found on her phone and had to fight not to react.

*I'm sorry I left mad. I don't want to stay in a fight with you. Please call me back. I want to—"* The crash and the horrible sound of breaking glass and rending steel would be etched in her brain forever.

Searching for a calm she didn't really feel, Emerson pulled on all her acting skills to modulate her voice. "You were in a car accident on your way back to school."

"I don't...quite remember."

"The doctor said that's normal. It may come back later." If it didn't, that was probably for the best. She didn't need more traumatic car crash memories.

"Were the cupcakes ruined?"

"Cup—" *Oh my God.* It was National Chocolate Cupcake Day. "That was why you came over. We were supposed to bake cupcakes. And I wasn't there."

The silly holiday had been strictly observed by Micah and Fiona. It had been something they could afford to celebrate on their meager budget, and every year they tried to outdo their previous outrageous creations. After her death, Emerson and Fi had continued the tradition as a way to keep her alive.

And this year Emerson had forgotten because she'd been thinking of no one but herself.

The guilt of that crumbled whatever tenuous control she'd cobbled together. The tears came fast and hard. She didn't even know exactly what she was weeping over. Relief that Fiona was alive. Grief that Micah wasn't. The overwhelming sense of failure that she'd missed something important to the child who was her everything. And the loss of a future she'd barely begun to embrace with a man she didn't think she'd ever get over. All of it made her feel like she was drowning, barely able to breathe.

Fiona squeezed her hand. "Please don't cry, Auntie Em. I'm sorry for putting you through this again."

That only made her sob harder because why should this precious child take the blame for any of this? Not when all of it lay squarely on Emerson's shoulders.

It took several tries to suck in enough breath and find enough control to force the words out. "Not on you. None of this is on you." If she could do nothing else, she could give Fiona this. "It's all my fault. Everything is my fault. I should have been there for you. Then and now."

"What?"

Her breath hitched. She'd never admitted this to another soul and saying it out loud now was like shoving a knife through her own heart. "Your mom died because of me."

"What are you talking about?"

"I didn't answer the phone that night when you called. I was out with friends at a bar and it was loud, and I figured I'd call you back later. If I'd answered, I would have come to get you, no question. Y'all would never have been where you were when that drunk asshole blew through the light. Micah would still be here."

Fiona began to cry.

"And tonight…I should have remembered. I was caught up in my own shit, but that's no excuse. I should have remembered and been there. I should never have let you walk out mad. We should have talked it out, like we always do. And we should have made triple chocolate cupcakes with some obnoxious, decadent twist that your mom would have loved. I should have been planning that for weeks. I shouldn't have been off galivanting with Caleb. I should have told you about him from the beginning. I should have trusted that we could all get through it." Losing track of all the things she was apologizing for, Emerson swallowed, trying to catch enough breath to keep speaking through the tears. "I'm sorry. I'm so fucking sorry for all of it. I won't mess up again. I won't leave you."

"It wasn't you."

She lifted her head to find tears tracking down Fiona's cheeks. "What?"

"It wasn't you, that night. Wasn't your fault. It was mine."

"What are you talking about?"

"If I hadn't been such a wimp, if I'd just stuck it out at that sleepover and not called her, nobody would have gotten hurt. If I hadn't called, she wouldn't have come. She wouldn't have died."

Oh. Oh God. Had this child really carried the guilt of that all these years?

Emerson struggled to pull herself together, to find some kind of rationale to battle this. "No. Don't you dare blame yourself. Your mom would never have wanted you to stick it out somewhere you were uncomfortable. Never. You can't blame yourself for that."

Fiona sniffed. "If I can't blame myself, then neither can you. I wasn't your responsibility. You didn't have to answer the phone."

That was technically true. But that didn't make it any easier to stop thinking of all the what ifs.

As if reading her mind, Fiona kept talking. "Caleb told me once that the what ifs are the hardest part when you're the one who survives. But that the only person at fault for the accident is the guy who chose to drive drunk. He got behind the wheel. He killed my mother. Not me. Not you. We don't get to hold on to that guilt. It's not our burden to bear."

Damn if that didn't make Emerson want to start sobbing again. Because even not here, Caleb was reaching out, making things just a little easier to handle.

"He's not wrong. That's hard to remember sometimes, in the moment, when I'm missing her so much." She sniffed and wiped at the tears. "I'm still sorry I missed Chocolate Cupcake Day."

"Can we have a do-over when I get out of here?"

She didn't know when that would be or how much Fi would be able to do with her arm and shoulder immobilized. But she'd make the world spin backward if that's what her girl needed.

"We can absolutely have a do-over."

And maybe on the other side of it, she'd figure out how to go back to her old life.

# CHAPTER 15

The glare of an overhead light had Caleb blinking awake, already halfway vertical on the sofa, hands curled to fists, before he spotted the intruder. Well, technically, he was the intruder.

Kyle stood in the entryway to his loft apartment, a guitar case at his feet and a duffel bag thrown over one shoulder. "You look like shit."

At least that's what Caleb thought he said. He couldn't actually hear the words past the audiobook still playing on his headphones. One of Emerson's, of course. It was the only way he'd been able to get any sleep since he'd given her what she wanted and walked away. Tugging out the earbuds, he scrubbed a hand over his head and squinted at his brother. "What the hell are you doing home? I thought you were in Maryland or some shit for the tour."

"There's a thirty-six-hour lag until our next performance. I got a notice from the security system when you got here, and when you didn't answer my calls, I figured I'd better come home to find out why the hell you came to my place and never left. Did something happen with Emerson?"

He gave a bitter laugh. "No. Nothing's happened with Emerson. It's been fucking two weeks, and she's still shutting me out."

Coming further into the room, Kyle eyed the empty whiskey bottle and takeout containers on the coffee table. "I feel like you're skipping some details. Last time I saw you two, everything was peachy."

"Yeah, well, last time I saw you, you swore there wasn't a chance in hell you'd get together with Mercy Lee Bradshaw, and there's that photo of your lip lock flying all over social media right now." Not that he'd given much of a shit about that due to his own personal circumstances.

Kyle scowled and prowled into his kitchen. "Fucking tabloids. That wasn't what it looked like. I swear to God, she ambushed me. But quit changing the subject. What happened with Emerson?" Grabbing a beer from the fridge, he held it up in invitation.

Caleb shook his head, feeling his brain bang against the confines of his skull. He'd had his night to get drunk off his ass. That was his rule. One and only one. The hangover had been fierce and still wasn't quite gone. He wouldn't do anything to add to it.

"I took her home for the reunion to meet the family."

"What? Like everybody?"

"Every last one. You were missed, by the way."

Kyle grunted. He rarely went home to Eden's Ridge, blaming it on his touring schedule and career commitments. But Caleb knew better.

"She was there, at the reunion."

"Yeah, you just said you took her."

"Don't play dumb. You know I'm talking about Abbey."

"Unless you're about to tell me she's spontaneously forgiven me, it's a moot point."

They were both so damned pigheaded.

"She might, if you'd man the fuck up and talk to her."

With admirable calm, Kyle dropped into a chair and propped

his booted feet on the edge of the coffee table. "We aren't talking about me and my mistakes. Quit avoiding the subject. Did the family scare Emerson off?"

Recognizing he wasn't going to get anywhere with his brother, Caleb dropped it. "No. In fact, the trip leveled us up in our relationship."

"Leveled you up how?"

"Talking about what we wanted. Commitment. A future together. A baby."

Kyle promptly sprayed his mouthful of beer and began to cough and wheeze. "A *baby?*"

If not for his own misery, the look of thunderstruck horror on Kyle's face might have made him smile. "I realize this is a shock to you, but some of us are actually thinking about settling down and having a family." He wanted that with every fiber of his being. Wanted to feel her belly growing round with their child beneath his hand. Wanted to marry her. He still wanted it all, on whatever timeline she was okay with.

Kyle retrieved a kitchen towel and began to mop up the mess. "Yeah, but isn't that getting ahead of things?"

Was it? Caleb hadn't felt like it at the time. The whole thing had felt like the natural evolution for them. They'd been on the same page when they got back from Eden's Ridge. He'd been sure of it. But maybe that had been wishful thinking.

"Doesn't matter. That wasn't the problem."

"What was, then?"

"Fiona was in an accident. She's all right. Or will be, once she's done healing. But the whole thing triggered Emerson. All the progress we'd made just—" He waved his hand. "—poof. She shut me out and shut me down. Like the last four years didn't happen. Said she couldn't do this anymore."

"'This' being…"

"Us, I guess. I know she was scared. I figured I'd back off like she wanted, and once she really knew Fi was okay, she'd settle down and come back. I kept tabs on them both through my contacts at the hospital."

"Creepy much?"

"Necessary. I needed to know they were okay, even if Emerson wouldn't let me close to help. But Fiona's out, home now. And other than a text to let me know that, Emerson hasn't said a damned word."

"You haven't seen them?"

"No. Fiona's texted me a few times, and I've put her off, saying I had to work. Used to be, I'd have just walked on over to check on them. But I don't feel like I can now. I don't know what kind of headspace Em is in, and I don't want to put her on the spot. So I'm stuck waiting." And he was beginning to wonder if he'd be waiting forever.

"And you're camped out at my place because why?"

"Because it's too fucking hard to be right next door and not just go over there. She wanted space, and I'm trying to give it to her."

Kyle studied him. "Bro, have you considered that 'I can't do this' doesn't count as 'I need space' in this instance? She might really be done."

Caleb shot to his feet. "No. She's not done. We're not done."

"How do you know?"

"Because I love her!" he exploded. "And she loves me."

"Has she said so?"

He opened his mouth to answer and shut it again. She'd never said the words. Not outright. But she wouldn't have been talking about having a child with him if she didn't love him. He wasn't just some anonymous sperm donor because she felt her biological clock ticking. She wouldn't have even been thinking in that direction if not for him changing things between them. She'd talked about a future and commitment. He'd been part of that fantasy she'd built. He refused to believe it was only that.

"She loves me," he repeated.

"And what if that's not enough? Sometimes it's not. Sometimes you can love somebody with everything you are and fuck it up or the timing is off or the damned planets never align. Sometimes fear is bigger than everything else."

What if he was right? What if she was too afraid to take a real chance on him, on them? If he hadn't proved to her by now that they could weather anything, would she ever believe it?

But Kyle wasn't talking about Emerson. He couldn't be. He was the one too chicken shit to face whatever had happened with Abbey, so he was projecting.

Caleb shook his head. "I can't believe that. Because if love isn't enough, then what the hell have I been doing with my life for the past four years?"

"Do you really want me to answer that?"

"Fuck you."

Caleb's phone vibrated with a text. He lunged for it on the table. But it wasn't Emerson's name on the screen. It was work.

"Multiple alarm fire. I'm being called in. I gotta go." Shoving on his shoes, Caleb made a fast pass through the room to grab up his essentials.

Kyle frowned. "Are you in any shape to be going out on the job?"

"I'm sober and I've worked through worse." Besides, if Emerson didn't change her mind, the job would be the only thing he had left.

"I'll be by to grab the rest of my stuff later. I know I didn't ask, but thanks for letting me crash here."

"No problem."

"You heading out tonight?"

"I'll go back tomorrow. Looking forward to sleeping in my own bed." He followed Caleb to the door, pausing to haul him in for a tight, back-thumping hug. "Be safe, brother."

Caleb squeezed back, grateful for his support, even if he was a pain in the ass. "Always."

Then he hauled ass to his truck and headed for the only part of his life that still made sense.

*  *  *

"THANKS FOR LETTING me come join for cupcakes. I'm between men at the moment, and I can absolutely use the chocolate pick-me-up."

Emerson worked up a smile for Paisley. She was grateful her friend had come to join in. It would help distract from her own relative lack of enthusiasm. If either of them asked, it would be easy to blame everything on exhaustion. As the stress of the accident and Fiona's surgery and subsequent recovery had settled over her like a fog, she'd just felt herself pulled down, down, down. All she wanted to do was sleep. Not that she was doing that, either. Lack of rest had her riding that faint edge of nausea that had been her normal for so long after Micah's death.

*Hello burnout, my old friend. I have not missed you.*

While the two of them worked on cupcake batter, Emerson took Mooch through his training. If her attention was on the dog, they were less likely to ask questions.

"Pass me the butter," Paisley ordered.

Fiona picked up the sticks of softened butter and handed them over. She was learning to manage with one arm in a sling and had, with Emerson's help, been working on making up her missed classwork. Her shoulder was healing well. Everything had stabilized in her life again.

And it all felt wrong without Caleb.

He hadn't come by. Why should he? She'd told him she was done. That she couldn't do a relationship anymore. But a part of her had still expected him to do what he'd always done and be what she needed despite her. But this go round she was getting none of the breaks. None of the support. She was starting to realize exactly how much she'd taken him for granted all this time.

She'd believed she'd been a single parent, but she hadn't. Not completely. He'd made himself so thoroughly a part of the fabric of their lives, she hadn't realized the extent to which he'd impacted the warp and weft of it until that thread had been yanked out—by her—wrecking everything.

Fiona perused the selection of fun-sized candy they'd gathered for stuffing and topping the cupcakes as Paisley finished mixing the batter.

"We should do Rolos for the caramel."

Emerson circled her finger in the air and Mooch flopped on his back and rolled over. She tossed him a tiny piece of Pupperoni. "You don't like caramel."

"But Caleb does. He's been working so much overtime lately, I thought we could take some to the station."

For the first time all night, Emerson really tuned in to the conversation. "How do you know that?"

Fiona shot her a sideways glance. "I've texted him. He said that's why he hasn't been by to see me."

Was that true? He didn't seem to be home, and she'd sure as hell looked. Not that she'd gone over there. Seeing him right now would be too damned hard. She'd thought maybe he felt the same and was avoiding them both. Maybe he had picked up some extra shifts. But there were limits to how much he could legally work before he absolutely had to have downtime for safety's sake.

Cupcakes would be a nice gesture and a way for Fiona to get her own relationship with him back on track to something resembling normal. No reason for her to suffer because of Emerson's stupidity.

"You're welcome to take some to him."

Fi frowned. "Why wouldn't you go?"

This wasn't something she wanted to talk about. But keeping her mouth shut was part of how they'd gotten here in the first place. Might as well be honest. "I don't think he wants to see me right now."

"Why not?

"We broke up." Admitting it out loud made her stomach lurch, and the little bit of dinner she'd managed earlier threatened to come back up.

Paisley narrowed her eyes in a glare Emerson knew entirely too well. "We or you?"

No point in denying the truth. "Me."

"Why?" The question wasn't delivered in the accusatory tone she'd expected, so it was somewhat easier to answer.

"I just realized I don't have the bandwidth for a relationship. We were getting in too deep, too fast, and I couldn't..." She trailed off, taking a breath to ward off the tears that were never far away. "Fiona has to be my priority."

"Wait, hold the phone. Why am I the reason? Did you suddenly miss the fact that I'm eighteen?"

The return of her sass made Emerson feel an iota better. "I didn't miss anything. You are my everything, and I won't put you in another situation where you're at risk."

Fiona stared at her. "How the hell does you not being with Caleb keep me from being at risk?"

"You were upset we were involved. You left here upset that night and weren't fully paying attention to the road. That's on me."

"What the actual fuck?" Fi exploded.

"Language," Emerson warned.

"No. Seriously. I wasn't upset you were dating Caleb. Why would I be? You two are perfect together. I totally pushed him into making sure you were okay after I left in hopes he'd finally do something about it."

Emerson's mouth fell open. "You...what? But...I don't understand. If you wanted him to make a move, why were you upset?"

"Because you didn't tell me about it! The same way Mom didn't tell me about her guy."

"Wait, wait. Micah was involved with someone?"

"Yeah. For a couple of years before the accident, I think. I never met him. Never even knew his name. I heard her on the phone with him once, and I think he really wanted to escalate their relationship but she wouldn't do it because of me. What the hell is up with the grown-ups in my life thinking I can't handle them having relationships with somebody other than me?"

Emerson's brain reeled at the idea that Micah had been dating someone. "She never told me. Not a word."

"I don't know why she didn't tell anybody. I think she worried about being judged."

"Or maybe she wanted to keep her life compartmentalized," Paisley suggested.

As Emerson had. "Mom life versus woman life," she murmured. "Sometimes it's hard to merge the two."

"Oh bullshit." Paisley dropped the batter scoop into the bowl with a wet thunk. "The idea that they aren't one and the same is some idiocy propagated by the patriarchy. Women are brainwashed into believing their only value is in being human givers, never allowed to be human beings with wants and desires and dreams of their own. They keep subjugating their needs beneath everyone else's and are quietly suffocating because they're giving away all of themselves. Is that *really* the behavior you want to model for Fiona?"

"I'm not—"

"Except you are. Don't you remember what she said on move in day? That she's not having kids because she can't possibly live up to the example you set."

Emerson had been flattered at the time, happy to have the validation for everything she'd done. But now... She looked to her daughter. "That's not what you meant, though. Is it?"

Fiona shrugged her uninjured shoulder. "I can't imagine being the kind of parent you've been. Or Mom, either. You've both given so much to me, and I can't fathom doing that. I have too many things I want to do, places I want to go. And I want love. If I can't have it all, I want that."

Heart twisting so hard it ached, Emerson pressed a hand to her chest. "You think you can't have love and career and family?"

"I mean…it's not exactly the norm in our society. And I definitely haven't had up close and personal examples. It seems like you can do one or two things well, but not everything."

Emerson opened her mouth to argue and, seeing Paisley's pursed lips, shut it again. Wasn't that exactly what she was telling Fiona with her own actions? She hadn't been transparent about the relationship in the first place, and at the first major challenge, she'd balked, leaning into fear instead of into Caleb. Not trusting in the relationship they'd developed. Because she'd drunk the Kool-aid that she had to be one or the other and choosing anything other than her child simply didn't compute.

"The fact is, kid, you can have everything. But not all by yourself. You can have kids and career if you have the love, if that love is a partnership, where you prop each other up in your weak spots and make a stronger unit together. Which is what I *thought* Emerson was building with Caleb." Paisley's expression was caught somewhere between disgust and pity. "You weren't supposed to be the dumbass in this love story. You narrate romance, for Pete's sake. You're supposed to know better. To recognize the unicorn and appreciate him for the awesome rarity of his kind, not throw him away."

Emerson had thrown him away. All the hundreds of tiny, thoughtful gestures, all the ways he'd made her life and Fiona's better. She'd squandered them all. He'd given her nothing but constancy and love, and she'd rejected him.

Tears erupted hot and fast, spilling down her face as her shoulders shook.

Fiona glared at Paisley as she moved over to wrap her good arm around Emerson's shoulder. "Too much. You broke her."

"No. She broke herself. This is part of the process. She recognizes that she fucked up. Once she's had a good cry, then we brainstorm how she's going to fix it."

"I don't...think...it can...be...fixed," Emerson hiccuped.

"Do you love him?"

"Yes."

"Do you still want a life with him?"

More than anything. "Yes."

"Then there's a better-than-average chance we can repair the damage."

"Do you really think he'll forgive me?"

"That man is hopelessly in love with you, and two weeks of you being an idiot shouldn't be enough to erase more than four years of devotion. And if it is, he isn't the unicorn I believe him to be." Paisley moved to the freezer and pulled out the Moose Tracks ice cream. "We don't have time to wait for the cupcakes. Fi, grab the tissues."

They huddled around her with ice cream and Kleenex as she cried herself dry. Emerson didn't eat much of the ice cream, but she appreciated the gesture and the feeling of unity. When she'd finished her weeping, she mopped her face. Someone shoved a bottle of water in her hand.

"Okay, oh wise one, how are we going to fix this?"

Paisley finally slipped the cupcakes in the oven. "Traditionally, the bigger the screw up, the bigger the grand gesture. How do you feel about flash mobs?"

Emerson was saved from replying to *that* ludicrous suggestion by the ringing of her phone. Snatching it up, her heart fell the moment she saw it wasn't Caleb's name on the screen. Not recognizing the number, she almost sent it to voicemail, but some niggling sense had her hesitating. Pushing past the whisper of unease, she hit answer.

"Hello?"

"Emerson?"

"Yes?"

"It's Kyle Keenan."

That threw her. Why on earth was Caleb's brother calling her? "How did you get my number?" Realizing that sounded a little rude, she backtracked. "Sorry. I wasn't expecting to hear from you."

She expected him to laugh a little, maybe make a joke. The silence on the line spun out two beats. Three. In the background she heard the muted sound of a PA system. Though she didn't catch actual words in the announcement, she recognized the tone —that brisk, neutral professionalism that saved and shattered lives behind a thin screen of medical jargon and codes.

The whisper inside her turned into a scream. Her fingers tightened around the phone. "Kyle, what's going on?"

"I—Listen, I know things between you and Caleb are weird right now but...I had to call you. I didn't want you to find out from somewhere else."

Her voice shook and the blood drained from her face, already anticipating the blow. "Find out what?"

He sucked in a long breath. "There's been an accident."

# CHAPTER 16

*E*merson's voice pulled Caleb up from the murky depths of fragmented dreams. He listened for a moment but couldn't make himself focus on the words of the book he'd gone to sleep to. He'd have to start it over again because he'd obviously slept through the beginning. But moving felt like a whole helluva lot of effort.

Everything hurt. His head felt like a gong, vibrating with pain, and he wasn't entirely sure some sadist hadn't performed a body transplant and attached his head to the body of an eighty-something old dude. What the hell kind of hangover was this? Had he broken his rule? He had dim memories of Kyle giving him shit and some lousy advice. Had they gotten shit-faced? He couldn't remember.

It wasn't worth the effort to stop the book. He'd just start it over later. Now, he'd sleep. Sleep would sweep away the hangover —at least for a little while.

Except, there was that beeping. What was that? Answering machine? Did anybody even have those anymore? Was it an alarm for something? Maybe the batteries needed changing in the smoke alarm or the carbon monoxide detector. In which case, he was fucked because climbing a ladder right now felt about as doable as climbing Everest.

"I don't know how to do this without you, Caleb."

The sound of his own name in that tear-choked voice had him stopping the sink back into oblivion. That wasn't part of a book.

"I made it through the last two times because you were there. Even when I tried to push you away, you stuck by me. But I don't know how to do this on my own. Not when you're the one who was hurt."

Hurt? What the hell was she talking about?

Flashes of memory lit up his brain like strobe lights. A fire. Breaching the building. Combing the halls of the upper floors looking for victims. Roof caving. Then nothing.

Maybe this headache wasn't from alcohol.

Caleb fought to move past it, but the weight of the ache was like trying to shove a locked steel door with his bare hands.

"The doctors say it's good that you're unconscious. That the body heals better that way. But are they really going to say anything else? It's a reality that there's a point where the sleep isn't healing. Where the longer you're out, the greater the chance you won't wake up. They won't tell me where you fall on that continuum. Hell, it's not like they're telling me anything at all. If not for Kyle, I'd be completely in the dark. He's gone home to shower. But he'll be back."

Huh. How the hell long had he been out?

"You'll probably be pissed at him for telling me. Actually, if he hadn't, Pru would have called me. They've all kept in close touch. But don't be angry with them. If you're going to be pissed at anybody, be pissed at me. I deserve it. At this point, I'd welcome you yelling at me. The deal is, you have to wake up to do it."

Caleb could sense movement off to his left. There was a faint whisper of a touch, a ripple along the bed, as if she'd pressed a hand into the mattress just beside his hand. Or where he thought his hand was. He couldn't quite tell where his edges were at the moment. But why wouldn't she touch him?

"I don't know what to do with your silence since Fi's accident. And that's so stupid. You were just doing what I asked." She sucked in a shaky breath. "I wish you hadn't listened to me. The last couple of weeks have been awful. I can't sleep. Don't want to eat. Sometimes it's even hard to breathe. I kept thinking you'd come through the back door and tell me time was up and we were going to talk about this. It's what I should have done instead of pushing you away."

She'd have been okay with that? Damn it, he'd miscalculated. He should have indulged himself. Should have gone over. Made her face what was between them. Instead, he'd stayed away, and now he was here in what was apparently a hospital bed, and his fucking body didn't want to cooperate.

"I know I hurt you. All you've ever been is wonderful to me. The truth is, Fiona's accident terrified me. It felt like this big warning from the Universe—don't dream too big. Don't forget your responsibilities. Don't think you can have it all because I can take it all away in a blink."

*You* can *have it all. I'm going to give it to you. If only you'll let me.*

Her voice softened. "I got scared. I thought it would be easier to go back to doing everything alone because I didn't risk as much. But I realized by sending you away, I was risking everything. Since you came into my life, I've never been truly alone. Because you were always, always there. I didn't recognize how much I counted on that, trusted in that, until you weren't there. And I've hated every minute of it."

*Me too.* Caleb flexed his lips, trying to get them around the words. But Emerson kept going.

"Paisley and Fiona already reamed me for being an idiot. We were working on a plan for how to fix it. According to Paisley, the level of the grand gesture required is directly proportionate to the level of stupid perpetrated by the offending party. She was talking flash mob when Kyle called. Seriously. Can you imagine that happening outside the fire station?"

There was an edge of smile in her voice. Not a real one. But that fake, I'm-trying-to-hold-my-shit-together-and-keep-talking-because-the-silence-and-the-beep-of-monitors-is-too-scary smile. Caleb held on to that sound as he fought to lift the concrete slabs impersonating his eyelids.

"It's totally crazy. You've met me. I can't dance. And yet, I'd do it for you without hesitation. I'll do anything for you, if only you'll wake up. I can't—" Her voice hitched, throat clogged with more tears. "I can't lose you. And I need you to fucking wake up so I can tell you all this properly. I need you to wake up so I can tell you how much I love you and beg you to forgive me."

She loved him. He'd known it, deep down, but now she'd said it and the words were like a power boost in a video game. Light and energy rushed along his limbs, helping him fight back the darkness that wanted to drag him back down. Some monitor beeped a little faster. He was going to break the fucking surface if it was the last thing he did because Emerson loved him and she needed to know he was here and okay.

His eyes opened to slits. The blurry swatch of room didn't tell him much, but he recognized Emerson's shape hunched over the side of his bed, crying, with her face pressed into the mattress.

With herculean effort, he shifted his fingers the couple of inches over to where hers curled on the blanket, hooking the pinky that weighed eight tons over hers.

Emerson bolted upright. "Caleb?"

"Mar—" His voice sounded like a rusted-out transmission grinding gears. Swallowing against the cotton in his throat, he tried again. "Marry You."

"What?" she gasped.

"Bru—no Mars. For the flash...mob."

Then she was laughing and crying and pressing kisses to his bandaged hand. "You're awake. Oh thank God, you're awake." Her words poured out in a flood. "I'm sorry. I'm so fucking sorry for everything. I love you. I should have told you before, but I'm telling you now. I love you. And if you want a flash mob with Bruno Mars' 'Marry You', then I'll find a way to pull that off."

Caleb tried to grin at that. His head felt like it was going to tip off its axis any moment now, but Emerson Aldridge loved him. He could survive anything knowing that. "Would be fun. But just want to actually marry you. How's next week?"

Emerson stared down at him. "Are you seriously coming out of a coma proposing?"

A coma? Shit, that was probably bad. But he'd sort that out later. This was more important. "Not letting you get away again."

More tears glimmered in her eyes. But there was something else there, too. Something that looked a lot like hope. "It's not fair of me to say yes. You have a head injury."

He scowled and instantly regretted it as pain rippled across his face and skull. "It's not the head injury. I love you."

Very gently, Emerson cupped his cheek, her slightly blurry faces resolving into one. "I love you, too."

"Say yes."

"Caleb."

"Marry me, Emerson. I still want the fantasy. Tell me you do, too."

"Yes." Her throat worked as she swallowed. "But if you change your mind after the concussion heals, I'll understand."

"I'm not changing my mind." And as soon as he got out of here, he was going shopping for a ring. Maybe Kyle would drive. "How long have I been out?"

"Forty-six hours and twenty-odd minutes. I would just like to go on record that nobody else ever gets to tell me 'There was an accident' again. I have reached my lifetime quota of being scared shitless."

"That's fair." He hoped like hell the Universe got the memo.

"I should get the doctor." She pressed the call button, then leaned over, brushing a soft kiss over his dry, cracked lips. "I love you, Caleb."

He was still grinning as the door opened behind her.

Emerson turned to address the newcomer. "He's awake!"

A nurse hurried around to the other side of the bed. "Welcome back, Mr. Romero."

"She said yes."

The nurse paused, glancing from him to Emerson. "Who said yes to what?"

"Emerson said she'd marry me."

Another look at Emerson. "Congratulations."

"I want it in my chart, on record. No takesies backsies."

The strict mask of professionalism cracked. "I'll see what I can do."

* * *

"WE COULD SKIP THE PARTY." Caleb's voice dropped into that sexy, cajoling tone that told Emerson exactly what he thought they should be doing instead.

Grateful she had something to occupy her hands, she put on some earrings and hoped he didn't notice the shaking in her hands. "We are not skipping the party. Everybody wants to see you hale and hearty, even if you haven't been cleared for full duty yet. It's good for station morale." That was her story, and she was sticking to it. At least until they got there and the plan she'd been working on for weeks finally unfolded.

Emerson hoped like hell it went off the way she'd planned.

Caleb slid his hands around her waist, pulling her back against his chest and brushing a kiss to the side of her neck. "Staying home would be good for *my* morale. I got cleared for that, too."

"I am aware." She'd lost count of all the let's-play-doctor jokes he'd been making since she brought him home from the hospital to convalesce.

He could have moved back into his own place after the first couple of weeks, but neither of them wanted that. More and more of his stuff had migrated over in the weeks since. Between him and Fiona, she had a full house—and for now, she liked it that way. The people she loved were safe and healing. It would be a while before she'd be able to let go of her Mother Hen routine. The hyper-vigilance left her exhausted most of the time. But that would fade as everything settled back to their new normal. And after the holidays, she really needed to get a handle on this whole self-medicating with ice cream thing before she had to buy all new pants.

In response to the pout, she pivoted in the circle of his arms, framing his face. "Later. If you're not too tired."

"I'm never too tired." His tone was full of promise as his hands skimmed down to curve around her ass.

"You were in *a coma* a matter of weeks ago." Emerson was pretty sure the whole ordeal had shaved more years off her life than his.

"It was less than two days. That was practically a nap."

She stared him down, pointing to her face. "You see this face? This is my not amused face." As he opened his mouth to argue, she shifted the point to him. "And don't you dare say it was just a bump on the head."

The double-barreled dimples flashed. "If I pretend to be more of an invalid, will you be my naughty nurse?"

Fiona's voice sounded from down the hall. "Quit trying to talk her into bed. Party now, bang later."

That put an effective stop to Caleb's wheedling. "I think maybe I liked it better when she didn't know we were together."

"There were definitely benefits. Come on. We're going to be late."

"You sure you want to wear that ivory dress? The chances of the menu consisting of chili, barbeque, spaghetti, or some other food involving a tomato-based sauce is high."

"I'm living on the wild side." She turned away before he could look closer and see the nerves. Pulling this whole thing off depended on her keeping cool, calm, and collected and him not suspecting a thing.

Downstairs, Fiona was already headed for the garage. "I'm driving myself. Meet you there!"

"Should she be doing that?" Caleb asked.

"The doctor cleared her to drive. She's got to start sometime, and I'd rather her do it on a three-mile stretch in town than all the way cross Nashville. She's so happy to be out of the sling, finally." Plus, if things went according to plan, she'd be spending the night elsewhere tonight.

"I'll get Mooch his treat ball." He started to move toward the back door.

"Already taken care of while you were in the shower. He's out back. I don't want to get him all riled up again before we go. Let's just slip on out. We won't be gone too late."

Assured Fiona had enough lead time on them to smuggle in her cargo, Emerson headed for her own car.

"I can drive, you know," he told her.

"Of course you can." No way was she letting him drive. She needed the steering wheel to grip so that he didn't take her hands and find them sweaty.

When she slid into the driver's seat anyway, he huffed an annoyed sigh and got in on the passenger side. "You're going to have to let things go back to normal sometime, Emerson."

"I know. I know all my caution and hovering is chafing on you. I'm getting there. I promise."

He reached out to tuck the hair behind her ear, voice gentling. "I'm ready to really start my life with you."

She looked at him, heart tripping into a frantic gallop. Could he see the frenetic beat of it in her throat? "Me, too."

"We should talk about that. Really talk. Make plans. Pick a date for the wedding. Figure out if we want to stay in this house or if we need a bigger one for when we start that family. Decide when we want to start that family."

Emotion built in her chest, a hot ball lodging just under her breastbone, like a balloon hitting a ceiling. "I love you, Caleb. And we can talk about all of that. But right now, we have to get to this party."

"You must be really excited about firehouse cooking."

"Something like that." She put the car into gear and backed out of the driveway.

"I hope somebody made cake."

Emerson's lips twitched. "I feel certain there will be cake."

The drive to the station took forever and no time at all. She was praying the whole time that her antiperspirant didn't give out. As they pulled up, Caleb leaned forward with a frown.

"What the hell are they doing?"

Two engines were pulled out of their bays, with the larger ladder truck parked crossways in front of them, making a U of vehicles that gleamed in the winter sun and blocked the central bay.

"That's going to slow down response times," he muttered as she parked in the cluster of cars off to one side. "Somebody's ass is going to get chewed for that."

"I'm sure Cue Ball is around somewhere for you to ask about it." Proud that her voice sounded casual, Emerson slid out of the car, surreptitiously wiping her sweaty palms.

Caleb came around the car to join her, taking her hand as she'd known he would. They began to walk toward the cluster of vehicles. Emerson caught the wink of a face through one of the windows of the firehouse and gave a subtle thumbs up.

*Showtime.*

She tugged on his hand, interrupting his one-track march toward the engines. "Caleb."

He swung toward her, eyes full of questions. What little food she'd managed to force down past the nerves that had a death grip on her stomach threatened to come back up.

"What's wrong?"

Music started playing over a PA system. It took him two and a half seconds to recognize Bruno Mars' "Marry You". A smile spread over his face. "Did you seriously pull together a flash mob?"

She shook her head. "I need to ask you something." Clutching her skirt with her free hand, Emerson dropped to one knee. "Will you marry me?"

The expression of surprise, amusement, and absolute love was worth every second of anxiety over planning this. "I already asked you that. You said yes. They documented it in my chart at the hospital."

"You did. And they did. I want to know if you'll marry me today. Now."

She waved her hand and the ladder truck cranked up, pulling out of the way to reveal rows of white chairs marching down an aisle that ended at the open bay of the fire station. The chairs were full of their friends, his company, and a good chunk of his family. Kyle stood in a suit at the front, with Paisley on the opposite side. Fiona waited at the head of the aisle, holding Mooch's leash and a bouquet of flowers. The dog himself was decked out with a bowtie and a pillow with the rings tied on.

Caleb's jaw dropped, his eyes going wide. That. That right there was the money shot that said she'd pulled this insanity off without him suspecting a thing.

"You planned a *wedding?*"

She couldn't hold back the grin. "I mean...you did say you were in a hurry."

He yanked her to her feet and into his arms, covering her mouth in a searing kiss. The audience cheered.

Somebody shouted, "We haven't gotten to that part yet!"

In the ripple of laughter, he pulled back, pressing his brow to hers. "Yes."

"Your suit's in the trunk."

He raced for the car in a dead sprint that sparked more laughter. All the speed drills he'd engaged in for work meant he was suited up at the head of the aisle, shaking hands with the minister, less than five minutes later.

Whichever joker was in charge of the music cued up something that sounded suspiciously like the start of Jock Jams. "Y'all ready for this!" blasted out over the speakers, followed by a record scratch and a shouted, "Sorry!" that didn't sound sorry at all. The helpless giggles unraveled Emerson's nerves, so when the real music began to play and Fiona walked down the aisle, Mooch at her side, a calm settled over her. They'd taken so long to get here, and there'd been a lot of pain and patience. But as she made her way toward Caleb, she knew this was absolutely where she was supposed to be.

In deference to the fact that the company could be called out at any moment, the ceremony was fast, their vows brief and traditional, though no less heartfelt for the brevity. The moment the minister made the pronouncement of man and wife, Caleb dipped her back in a kiss that left her head spinning. Emerson really hoped somebody had gotten a picture of that.

"No takesies backsies, Mrs. Romero," he murmured.

Holy shit. They'd really done it. She'd really married her hot, younger, firefighter, best friend next door. And it felt glorious.

Tugging him to the side while everybody leapt into motion to shift the chairs, roll up the aisle and clear the path, just in case, she curled her hand in his. "I've got one more surprise for you."

"I saw the cake."

Somebody had added a firetruck topper with a little bride and groom peeking out either window.

"Not the cake. Although, it's red velvet."

His eyes kindled. "My favorite."

"I know." She reached into the bodice of her dress where she'd stuck the small card.

Pulling her closer, he peered down into her cleavage. "What else are you hiding in there?"

"You will have ample opportunity to find out tonight." Swallowing another little bump of nerves, she handed the card over. "Your sort of wedding present."

He skimmed it, clearly not understanding. "Okay, it's an appointment for something on Monday."

"Flip it over."

"Hamilton Women's Clinic." His eyes snapped to hers. "For your IUD?"

Linking her arms around his neck, she rose to her toes. "You waited forever for me. I figure it's time to get this party started."

He lowered his mouth to hers. "Hell, yes."

# EPILOGUE

"*Y*ou look way too excited to be here."

Not being on full duty meant Caleb had zero problem getting off work to go with Emerson to the doctor. He'd been grinning like an idiot since they walked in the door. Probably that was the newlywed haze. "I mean, I'm not the one who had to pee in a cup."

"Fair point."

But he was excited. As he looked around the waiting room at all the expectant mothers in various stages of pregnancy, some with partners, some with other small children in tow, all he could think was *This will be us soon. Hopefully.*

He wanted to be here next to Emerson as she grew round with their son or daughter. Wanted to hold her hand through all the exams, hang on to her purse, and all that couply stuff. This was where that life he wanted with family cookouts and T-ball games and kitchen dance-offs really began.

Well, technically no. He was really hoping they'd be starting that literal life on the honeymoon they still needed to plan. "So where do we want to go?"

"Your sisters offered us a suite at the inn as a wedding present."

"Sweet of them, but I don't think I can properly honeymoon in the house I used to live in as a teenager." He was thinking it would be a clothing optional situation, with proper privacy so he could worship every inch of his wife. His *wife*. He still couldn't get over the fact that it was real. That she'd actually planned a surprise wedding. And here they were to take the next big step in their life together. Once she made up her mind, Emerson was full steam ahead, and he was so here for it.

At the sound of a nurse calling her name, Emerson rose. They followed her down a winding hallway and into an exam room.

"The gown is on the table. Please undress. Dr. Naylor will be in shortly."

As the door shut, Caleb picked up the "gown" and unfolded it. "Did they accidentally pull out a drape for the dentist? Because this is not going to do much to cover you."

"Welcome to the indignities of being female. That would be why I brought the big purse." As he watched, she opened up the gigantic tote bag and extracted a robe. "I come with my own."

"Smart girl."

Rising to her toes, she kissed him. "You didn't just marry me for my pretty face."

"True enough. That ass was also high on my list." He gave it a squeeze.

Swatting at his hand, she disappeared behind a curtain in the corner.

Still chuckling, he leaned back against the exam table. "To get back to marriage and honeymoon, Porter has some rental cabins up in that area. It's off season, so there's a good chance one or more of them is available. Then we'd have plenty of privacy to indulge in every conceivable position of baby making."

The silence stretched out just a few beats too long.

"About that."

Oh damn. Had he gone too far down the path of enthusiasm?

Emerson drew the curtain back, stepping out in her thin, cotton robe. Her bottom lip was caught between her teeth.

Reeling in his excitement, he took her hands. "Hey, if you're changing your mind, that's okay. This is a lot really fast. We can put that off until later." He'd be disappointed, but damn, he didn't ever want her to think she wasn't enough on her own.

"No, it's not that. I'm ready to try. I just…we need to manage our expectations here. I *am* older. That is a biological fact. Even apart from the fact that my body will take time to adjust to the lack of hormones from the IUD, we need to be prepared for this to take a while. Or…to maybe not happen at all."

Wanting to put her at ease, he pulled her in. "I love you. Period. End of story. If having kids this way doesn't work out, then we can check out the alternatives. Or we can revisit not having them at all, if that's what we decide to do. This is not a dealbreaker for me, and it doesn't make me love you any less. So, right now, let's just be positive and hopeful, and if it takes a while, then we'll just be grateful for all the opportunities to get creative in bed. And anywhere else that strikes our fancy."

Her cheeks flushed, her eyes going bright. "Okay, yeah, you should talk to Porter about a cabin."

"Your wish is my command."

A perfunctory knock sounded, and the door opened. The doctor came in, her bright red hair a stark contrast to the white lab coat. "Emerson, hello again. And is this the father?"

Caleb blinked. Wasn't that getting ahead of things? Well, Emerson had listed conception and advanced maternal age as topics she wanted to discuss. Maybe Dr. Naylor was making assumptions based on the pre-appointment paperwork.

If Emerson was thrown by the question, she didn't show it. "Well, we haven't gotten there yet, but yes. This is my husband, Caleb Romero."

Hearing her call him "husband" made Caleb want to preen like a peacock. He held it down to a grin.

"Oh, you got married! Congratulations."

"Thank you." She perched on the end of the exam table. "We wanted to discuss the risks of my getting pregnant at this age and see what we'd be getting into before getting my IUD removed."

Dr. Naylor checked her chart. "We'll certainly need to remove it if it's still there."

Emerson frowned. "What do you mean, if it's still there? Of course it's there."

"Have you checked the strings recently?"

That seemed to fluster her. "I mean, no, but—"

"Strings?" Caleb asked.

"There are strings on the bottom of an IUD," Dr. Naylor explained. "They dangle partway down the vaginal canal. It's an easy way to check to make sure it's still in place or if it's shifted or been expelled."

He glanced at Emerson. "I...uh...haven't noticed any strings." And there'd been plenty of up-close-and-personal opportunity since he'd been cleared by his own doctors.

The doctor nodded, amusement curving her lips. "That would explain why you're pregnant."

Caleb dropped into the visitor's chair with a thud.

Emerson's jaw dropped. "I'm...*what?*"

He reached for her hand. "Best wedding present ever."

"I never...I thought...holy shit, I was not prepared for this. How...how far?"

"It's a little tough to pin down how far since your cycle has been inconsistent, so we'll do a confirmatory exam."

Head spinning, Caleb did his best to listen as the doctor performed the exam—her IUD had definitely been expelled at some point—and did the first ultrasound. But after she pointed out the yolk sac and the little lima-bean-sized alien in there, he didn't hear anything else.

A baby.

That was his son or daughter in there. *Their* son or daughter.

He'd dreamed of this, wanted this, but he hadn't quite let himself believe he could have it. Gratitude rose up through the sense of disbelief, and beneath it all, a love that would've sent him to his knees if he hadn't already been sitting.

As they heard the rapid swish of the heartbeat for the first time, Emerson's hand trembled in his and tears slid down her cheeks. "Caleb, we did it."

"Damn straight." Bursting with love and pride, he leaned in to kiss his wife. "I love you so damned much."

"The timeline may shift around a bit as you get further along, but right now my best guess is you're right at nine or ten weeks."

"Nine or ten weeks?" Emerson echoed. She met his gaze, her own full of tremulous emotion. "The reunion."

Caleb reached for her hand as he did the mental math himself. "Or the night we got back."

*What if I want a baby?*

God, he'd wanted to give her that so badly. He'd wanted to give her everything. And in that moment, it had all seemed possible. Maybe that wasn't so far from the truth.

Dr. Naylor finished up the exam, going over instructions and follow-up and nutritional recommendations. Then they were alone.

Emerson slid off the table, pressing one hand to her belly. "I can't believe we're pregnant." The corners of her mouth twitched. "You either have the world's most determined sperm or the most impressive powers of visualization known to man."

Snagging her around the waist, he pulled her in. "It could be both. I was thinking really, *really* hard about making a baby that night."

She wrapped her arms around him and laughed, and her joy was the best sound in the world. "So was I."

"Should we wait to tell Fiona?" With just a few more weeks until the end of the first trimester, it wouldn't be too long.

"You know what? No. Let's FaceTime her right now."

Delighted, he settled next to her against the exam table as she put in the call.

A few moments later, Fi's face filled the small screen. As she spotted both of them, her brows shot up. "Hey newlyweds! What's up?"

"So we have something to tell you," Emerson began.

"Where are you?"

"Doctor's office."

"Is everything okay? Because I can skip my afternoon class and—"

"Everything's fine. Better than fine." She took a breath. "You're going to be a big sister."

"Holy shit!" As soon as the words were out, Fiona's shoulders hunched and she mouthed an apology to someone nearby. "Gimme a second."

There was a blur of motion and about twenty seconds later the sound of a door.

"Okay, I'm outside now." She whooped again. "You're really pregnant?"

"So the doctor says."

"This is freaking *awesome!* I'm going to big sister the crap out of this kid! When are you due?"

"Mid-July."

"Perfect! I'll be between semesters and can help out. We've got to celebrate. Wait? What can you eat? Not eat? Never mind, I'll figure it out. This is *great!*"

"I'm glad you're excited. I need to get dressed so we can get out of here, but we wanted you to be the first to know."

Fi pressed a hand to her heart. "Awww. I love y'all."

"We love you, too, kid," Caleb said.

They said their goodbyes and Emerson moved to get dressed. "I guess the point of the honeymoon is kind of past now."

"Not a chance in hell. I still want a week alone with my wife. It'll just be a babymoon instead. That's a thing, right?"

"If it's not, we'll make it one. And we can put our mutually strong powers of visualization to work figuring out the rest of our happily ever after."

"That sounds like the perfect way to spend the rest of our lives."

Taking her hand, they stepped through the door to start it.

\* \* \*

CHOOSE YOUR NEXT ROMANCE

ADMIT IT. You're DYING to know what happened with Kyle and Abbey, aren't you? Their story is coming this summer.

Meanwhile, if you haven't yet checked out the original Misfit Inn quartet about Caleb's sisters, it begins with *When You Got A Good Thing,* Kennedy and Xander's story. This whole series is all about the family you make and the bonds between sisters.

If you're wanting another kind of band of brothers, check out my *Rescue My Heart* series. This trilogy follows three former Army Rangers navigating their post-military lives and finding love long the way. They're all friends of Porter's, so there are plenty of cameos from our Misfit Inn favorites. It all begins with *Baby It's Cold Outside.*

Can't decide? Keep turning the pages for a sneak peek of both!

# SNEAK PEEK WHEN YOU GOT A GOOD THING

## THE MISFIT INN, BOOK #1

*I*n the mood for more Eden's Ridge? Check out Sheriff Xander Kincaid's story!

**Charming, poignant, and sexy,** *When You Got a Good Thing* **pulled me in with its sweet charm and deft storytelling, and didn't let go until the very last page. It has everything I love in a small-town romance!** **~USA Today Best-Selling Author Tawna Fenske**

She thought she could never go home again. Kennedy Reynolds has spent the past decade traveling the world as a free spirit. She never looks back at the past, the place, or the love she left behind —until her adopted mother's unexpected death forces her home to Eden's Ridge, Tennessee.

Deputy Xander Kincaid has never forgotten his first love. He's spent ten long years waiting for the chance to make up for one bone-headed mistake that sent her running. Now that she's finally home, he wants to give her so much more than just an apology.

Kennedy finds an unexpected ally in Xander, as she struggles to mend fences with her sisters and to care for the foster child her mother left behind.   Falling back into his arms is beyond tempting, but accepting his support is dangerous.   He can never know the truth about why she really left. Will Kennedy be able to bury the past and carve out her place in the Ridge, or will her secret destroy her second chance?

"WELCOME TO O'LEARY'S PUB. What can I get you?" The greeting rolled off Kennedy Reynolds' tongue as she continued to work the taps with deft hands.

The man on the other side of the long, polished bar gaped at her. "You're American."

Kennedy topped off the pint of Harp and slid it expertly into a patron's waiting hand. "So are you." She injected the lilt of Ireland into her voice instead of the faint twang of East Tennessee. "You'd be expectin' somethin' more along these lines, I'd wager. So what'll it be for a strapping Yank like yourself?"

The guy only blinked at her.

So she wasn't exactly typical of County Kerry, Ireland. Her sisters would be the first to say she wasn't exactly typical of anyone, anywhere. It didn't bother her. But there was a line stacking up behind this slack-jawed idiot, and she had work to do.

"Can I suggest a pint of Guinness? Or perhaps you'd prefer whiskey to warm you through? The night's still got a bit of a chill."

He seemed to shake himself. "Uh, Jameson."

She poured his drink, already looking past him to take the next order, when he spoke again.

"How's a girl from—is that Texas I hear in there?—wind up working in a pub in Ireland?"

*This again? Really?* Kennedy repressed the eye roll, determined to be polite and professional

A big, long-fingered hand slapped the guy on the shoulder

hard enough to almost slosh the whiskey. "Well now, I suppose herself walked right in and answered the help wanted sign." The speaker shifted twinkling blue eyes to Kennedy's. "That was how it happened in Dublin, now wasn't it, darlin'?"

"And Galway," she added, shooting a grin in Flynn's direction. "I'd heard rumor you were playing tonight. Usual?"

"If you'd be so kind. It's good to see you, *deifiúr beag.*" His voice was low and rich with affection, the kind of tone for greeting an old lover—which was laughable. Flynn Bohannon was about as far from her lover as he could get. But it did the trick.

With some relief, Kennedy saw the American wander away. "Thanks for that."

"All in a day's work," Flynn replied.

"I've missed your pretty face." She glanced at the nearly black beard now covering his cheeks as she began to pull his pint of Murphy's Irish Stout. "Even if you are hiding it these days."

He grinned, laying a hand over his heart. "Self preservation, love."

"You keep telling yourself that." Kennedy glanced at the line snaking back through the pub. "I'm slammed here, and you're starting your set shortly. Catch up later?"

Flynn lifted the beer and toasted her before making his way toward the tiny stage shoehorned beside the fireplace, where the other two members of his trio were waiting.

Mhairi, one of the waitstaff, wandered over, setting her tray on the bar as she all but drooled in his direction. "Well now, I'd not be kickin' that one out of bed for eating crisps."

"Wait 'til you hear him play."

Mhairi glanced back at Kennedy, lifting a brow in question. "Are you and he…?"

"No. Just friends. The way there is clear, so far as I know."

The waitress smiled. "Brilliant." She reeled off orders and it was back to the job at hand.

As Kennedy continued to pour drinks, Flynn and his band tuned instruments. They weren't the same pair who'd been with him in Dublin, whom she'd traveled with for several weeks as an extra voice. That wasn't much of a surprise. It'd been—what?—a year or so since they'd parted in Scotland. Flynn would, she knew, go where the music took him. And that sometimes meant changing up his companions. He was as much an unfettered gypsy as she was, which was why they'd become such fast friends. But whereas he didn't mind a different city or village every night, she preferred to take a more leisurely pace, picking up seasonal work and staying put for two or three months at a stretch. Really immersing herself in the culture of a place. The ability to pause and soak in each new environment gave her both the thrill of the new and kept her from feeling that incessant, terrified rush of not being able to fit in everything she wanted to see or do. It was important to her to avoid that, to take the time to be still in a place and find out what it really had to teach her.

The itinerant lifestyle worked for her. She'd seen huge chunks of the world over the past decade, made friends of every stripe, picked up bits and pieces of more than a dozen languages. Many people saw her life as unstable. She preferred to think of it as an endless adventure. What did their stability give them? Consistent money in the bank, yes. But also boredom and stress and a suffocating sameness. No, thank you. Kennedy would take her unique experiences any day. Never mind that the desk jobs and business suits had never even been a possibility for her. She'd been ill-suited for the education that led to those anyway.

Across the pub, Flynn drew his bow across his fiddle and launched into a lively jig. The crowd immediately shifted its focus. Those who knew the tune began to clap or stomp in time, and a handful of patrons leapt up and into the dance. Kennedy loved the spontaneity of it, the unreserved joy and fun. As jig rolled into reel and reel into hornpipe, she found herself in her own kind of dance as she moved behind the bar. Flynn switched instruments with the ease of shaking hands, playing or lifting his voice as the tune dictated. He even dragged Kennedy in for a couple of duets that made her nostalgic for their touring days. His music made the night pass quickly, so she didn't feel the ache in her feet until she'd shut the door behind the last patron.

Flynn kicked back against the bar. "A good night, I'd say."

"A very good night," Kennedy agreed.

"Help you clean up?"

"I wouldn't say no."

They went through the motions with the other staff, clearing tables, wiping down, sweeping up. Mhairi went on home—disappointed. And Kennedy promised Seamus, the pub's owner, that she'd lock up on her way out. Then, at long last, she settled in beside the remains of the fire with her own pint.

Flynn lifted his. "To unexpected encounters with old friends."

"Why unexpected?"

"You said yourself you rarely stay more than three months in a place. You've already been from one coast of Ireland to the other. I didn't expect you back."

"I always seem pulled back here," she admitted. "The people. The culture. As a whole, I suppose Ireland has been as close as I've had to a home base over the past ten years. I've spent more collective time in this country than anywhere else combined since I started traveling."

"How long have you been in Kerry?"

"Coming up on three months."

"Thinking of settling?" he asked.

Was she? No. She still felt that vague itch between her shoulder blades that she got every time she'd been long enough in a place. She knew she'd be moving on soon, searching for the next place to quiet the yearning she refused to acknowledge. "Not exactly. I haven't decided where I want to go next. Which isn't the same thing." She took a breath and spilled out the news she'd told no one. "I've been contacted by a book editor in New York. She wants me to turn my blog into a book."

"Really?" Flynn's grin spread wide and sparkling as the River Liffey. "That's grand!"

It was the most exciting thing to ever happen to her, and she was glad to finally get a chance to share it. "I haven't said yes."

"Why not? Are the terms not to your liking?"

"We haven't gotten that far. I'm still thinking about it." Still looking for reasons to talk herself out of it.

"What's there to think about?" Flynn prodded.

"A book means deadlines and criticism and working on other people's schedules. None of those are exactly my strong suit."

"Bollocks. Every job you've had has been on someone else's schedule. As to deadlines, how hard can it be to take what you've already written and turn it into a book? *Not All Who Wander* is well-written, engaging, and personal. You're a talented writer."

On her better days, Kennedy could admit that. But it was one thing having her little travel blog, with its admittedly solid online following, be read and commented on via the anonymity of the internet. It was a whole other animal turning that into a book that lots of people could read. Or not read, as the case might be. That was opening herself up to a level of failure she didn't even want to contemplate.

"She's offered to fly me to New York to meet with her, and I'm thinking about taking her up on the offer. I might feel better about the idea of the project if we talk about it in person."

"And if you go back across the pond, will you finally take a detour home?"

At the mention of Eden's Ridge, Kennedy felt some of her pleasure in the evening dim. "It hasn't really been on my radar as an option."

"Maybe it should be."

She lifted a brow. "This from the man who's been on the go nearly as long as I have?"

"I travel and often, yes, but I've been home. I've seen my family. You've been running."

"I'm not running," she insisted.

"All right, not running. Searching, then. For something. In all your travels, have you found it?"

"How can I even answer that? I don't know what I'm looking for." But that was a lie. She knew what she was looking for and knew she wouldn't find it in any new country, on any new adventure.

"I'd say that's an answer in and of itself."

Kennedy scowled into her beer. "I've had my reasons for staying away from home."

"They aren't family. You've seen them since you left. So who?"

Her gaze shot to his.

Flynn jerked his shoulders and gave an easy smile. "Deduction, *deifiúr beag.* Who was he?"

*Someone better off without me.*

She was saved from answering by the ringing of her mobile phone. "Late for a call." Fishing it out of her pocket, she saw her mother's number flash across the screen. "Not so late back in Tennessee." She hit answer. "Hey, Mom."

"Kennedy."

At the sound of her name, she felt her stomach clench into knots. Because it wasn't her mother, and the strain in her eldest sister's voice was palpable. "Pru?"

"Are you sitting down?"

Absolutely nothing good could follow those words. "What?"

Beside her, Flynn straightened, setting his pint to the side.

"You're not on the street where you can accidentally walk into traffic or something are you?"

"I'm sitting. What the hell is going on? Where's Mom?"

Her sister took a shaky breath. "Kennedy, Mom was in an accident. Her car was in the shop, and she was in a loaner. We've had a cold snap."

"What?" Kennedy whispered.

"She…" Pru gave a hiccuping sort of sob. "She didn't make it."

The earth fell out from beneath Kennedy's chair, and she curled her hand tighter around the phone, as if that pitiful anchor would help. She didn't even recognize her own voice as she asked, "Mom's dead?"

She wasn't aware of Flynn moving, but suddenly he was there, his strong hand curling around hers.

"The doctors said it was all but instant. She didn't suffer. I…we need to make arrangements."

"Arrangements." She needed to get the hell off the phone. She needed to move, to throw something, to rail at the Universe because this…this shouldn't be happening. "I have to go."

"Kennedy, I know this is hard but—"

"I'm coming home. I'll be there absolutely as soon as I can. Call you back as soon as I know when." She hung up before Pru could answer.

"Do you want me to come with you?" Flynn asked.

He would. He'd cancel whatever bookings he had and fly across an ocean with her to face the grief and demons that waited in Eden's Ridge. But this was for her to do.

"No. I… No." Lifting her eyes to his, she felt the weight of grief land on her chest like a boulder. She'd never again hear her mother's laugh. Never smell her mother's favorite perfume. Never get a chance to tell her the truth about why she'd walked away. "Flynn."

Without word, without question, he tugged her into his arms, holding tight as the first wave crashed over her, and she fell apart, the phantom scent of violets on the air.

CHIEF DEPUTY XANDER KINCAID parked his cruiser in front of the rambling Victorian that had been Joan Reynolds' home. He retrieved the covered dish of chicken enchiladas sent by his mama —the first wave of death casseroles that would soon fill the old kitchen to bursting—and headed for the front door. Despite its size, with its muted gray paint, the house tended to blend into the woods and mountains around it. Joan had loved this house. She'd always said it was a peaceful spot, a good place to heal and a good place to love. And she'd done exactly that for nearly twenty-five of her sixty-two years, filling the over-sized house with foster children who'd needed a home and someone to love them.

No telling whose home it would become now. Pru had moved back in. As the only one of Joan's adopted girls who hadn't moved away, she'd immediately stepped in to take over guardianship of Ari Rosas, Joan's most recent—well, her last foster child. But he didn't imagine Pru could afford the upkeep of the place on her income as a massage therapist—especially after the death taxes and probate lawyer had their way with the place. And what, he wondered, would happen with Ari, whose adoption hadn't yet been finalized?

Juggling the casserole dish, he rang the bell and waited. And waited.

Backing up on the porch, he craned his head to peer around toward the barn. Pru's car was there. He tried the knob and found it unlocked. Making a mental note to have a word with her about security, even here on the Ridge, he stuck his head inside. "Pru?"

She appeared at the head of the stairs, her big brown eyes red-rimmed from crying. "Sorry. I was just..." She tailed off, waving a vague hand down the hall.

"It's fine." He lifted the enchiladas. "Mama wanted me to bring these by. She thought with your sisters coming in, the last thing you or any of them would want to do is cook."

Xander watched as manners kicked in. Her posture straightened, her expression smoothing out as she locked down the grief.

"That's so kind of her." She came down the stairs and reached for the dish. "I'll just go put this in the kitchen."

He followed her back.

"No one's here just yet," she said, a false bright note in her voice, as if everything was fine and her world wasn't falling apart.

Xander waited until she slid the casserole into the fridge before he simply wrapped his arms around her. "Pru. I'm so sorry."

For a long moment, she stood there like a wooden post. Then a shudder rippled through her as her control fractured. Her arms lifted and she burrowed in.

"This shouldn't have happened," she whispered. "If she'd been in her own car instead of that tin can loaner, it wouldn't have."

Xander wasn't sure Joan's SUV would've handled the patch of black ice any better, but he remained silent. The fact was, nobody expected black ice in east Tennessee in March. Not when daytime temperatures were almost to the sixties. Joan's hadn't been the only accident this week. But she'd been the only fatality.

He ran a hand down Pru's silky, dark brown hair, hoping to soothe, at least a little. But this wasn't like middle school, when he'd been able to pound Derek Pedretti into the ground for making Pru cry by calling her fat. There was no one he could take to task, no one to be punished. Grief simply had to be endured.

"There are all these arrangements to be made," she hiccupped.

And no one here to help her do them, with Maggie off in Los Angeles and Athena running her restaurant in Chicago. Xander deliberately avoided thinking about the final Reynolds sister, though he was sure that this would bring even her home. The idea of that caused his gut to tighten with a mix of old fury and guilt.

"What can I do to help?"

"Let me make you some coffee."

"Pru—"

"No really," she sniffed, pulling away. "I'm better when I'm doing something."

Xander didn't want coffee, but if she needed to keep her hands busy, he'd drink some. "Coffee'd be great."

She began puttering around the kitchen, pulling beans out of the freezer and scooping them into the grinder. Joan had loved her gourmet beans. It'd been one of the few luxuries she'd always allowed herself. As she went through the motions, Pru seemed to regain her control.

"Maggie's taking the red eye from LA, and Athena's flying out as soon as she closes down the restaurant tonight."

"Do either of them need to be picked up from the airport?"

"They're meeting in Nashville and driving up together in the morning, so they'll be here to help me finish planning the service. It's supposed to be on Thursday."

Xander didn't ask about Kennedy. Both because he didn't want to care whether she showed up, and if she wasn't coming, he didn't want to rub it in.

Pru set a steaming mug in front of him, adding the dollop of half and half he liked and giving it a stir. "Kennedy gets in day after tomorrow. There was some kind of issue getting a direct flight, so she's having to criss-cross Europe before she even makes it Stateside again. She's coming home, Xander."

He wasn't sure if that was supposed to be an announcement or a warning, but it cracked open the scab over a very old wound that had never quite healed.

She laid a hand over his. "Are you okay?"

This woman had just lost her mother, and she was worried about whether he'd be okay with the fact that his high school girlfriend, whom he hadn't seen in a decade, was coming home.

"Why wouldn't I be?"

Pru leveled those deep, dark eyes on his. "I know there are unresolved issues between you."

God, if only she knew the truth—that he was the reason Kennedy had left—she wouldn't be so quick to offer sympathy.

"It was a long time ago, Pru. There's nothing to resolve."

Kennedy had made her position clear without saying a word to him. At the memory, temper stirred, belying his words. There were things he needed to say to her, questions he wanted answered. But whatever her faults, Kennedy had just lost her mother, too, and Xander wasn't the kind of asshole who'd attack her and demand them while she was reeling from that. Chances were, she'd be gone before he had an opportunity to say a thing. He'd gotten used to living with disappointment on that front.

He laid a hand over Pru's. "Don't worry about me. How's Ari?"

She straightened. "Devastated. Terrified. And..." Pru sighed. "Not speaking."

"Not speaking?"

"Not since I told her. She'd come so far living here with Mom, and this is an enormous setback. No surprise. Especially having just lost her grandmother last year." Pru continued to bustle around the kitchen, pouring herself a cup of coffee and coming to sit with him at the table. Her long, capable fingers wrapped around the mug.

"She upstairs?"

"Yeah. I was trying to get her to eat something when you got here."

"Poor kid. Have you talked to the social worker yet?"

"Briefly. Mae wants to let us get through the funeral and all the stuff after before we all figure out what to do."

"Who would've been named her emergency guardian if the adoption had gone through?" Xander asked.

"The four of us, probably. I know it's what Mom would've wanted. But there are legal ramifications to the situation, and the fact is, I'm the only one still here." She sighed. "We'll have to talk about it after. The one thing I know we'll all be in agreement on is that we want what's best for Ari."

"All four of you have been in her shoes, and you turned into amazing women. I know you'll do the right thing." Whatever that turned out to be.

Xander polished off the coffee. "I'm on shift, so I need to be getting back. But, please, if you need *anything*, Pru, don't hesitate to call. I'm just down the road."

She rose as he did and laid a hand on his cheek. "You're a good stand-in brother, Xander. Mom always loved that about you."

He felt another prick of guilt, knowing his own involvement with this family had been heavily motivated by trying to make up for Kennedy's absence. "Yeah well, I ran as tame here as the rest of you when we were kids. Especially when Porter was around." Giving her another squeeze, he asked, "Can I do that for you? Notify the rest of her fosters? I know you've covered your sisters, but there were a lot of kids who went through here over the years. I'm sure they'd like to pay their respects."

Her face relaxed a fraction. "That would be amazing. I'm sure we'll have a houseful after the funeral, but I need a chance to gird my loins for the influx. Mom kept a list. I'll get it for you."

As she disappeared upstairs, he wandered into the living room. Little had changed over the years. The big, cushy sofas had rotated a time or two. And there'd been at least three rugs that he could remember. But photos of Joan and her charges were scattered everywhere. Xander eased along the wall, scanning faces. A lot of them he knew. A lot of them, he didn't.

A shot at the end caught his attention. The girl's face was turned away from the camera, looking out over the misty mountains. She was on the cusp of womanhood, her long, tanned legs crossed on the swing that still hung from the porch outside, a book forgotten in her lap. Her golden hair was caught in a loose tail at her nape. Xander's fingers itched with the memory of the silky strands flowing through his fingers. She'd been sixteen, gorgeous, and the center of his world. The sight of her still gave him a punch in the gut.

"Here it is."

At the sound of Pru's voice, Xander turned away from Kennedy's picture. *Over and done.*

He strode over and took the pages she'd printed. "I'll take care of it," he promised.

"Thank you, Xander. This means a lot."

"Anytime." With one last, affectionate tug on her hair, he stepped outside, away from memories and the looming specter of what might have been.

GET **your copy of** *When You Got A Good Thing* **today!**

# SNEAK PEEK BABY, IT'S COLD OUTSIDE

## RESCUE MY HEART BOOK #1

**A grumpy lumberjack**

Former Army Ranger Harrison Wilkes isn't actually a lumberjack, but he's doing his best impression while hiding out in the mountains of East Tennessee. He needs to rest, recharge, and stay the hell away from people, while he wrestles with ghosts from his past and figures out his future. Neither includes a snowbound rescue of his favorite author.

**A runaway writer**

Ivy Blake is on a deadline. Her hero is MIA, and she's desperate to find some peace, quiet, and inspiration to get her book—and her life—back on track. She doesn't plan on driving off a mountain. Or the mysterious stranger who shows up to save her.

**Who's rescuing who?**

When Winter Stormageddon traps them together, Ivy finds the inspiration she didn't know she needed in her real-life hero. As more than the fireplace heats up his one-man cabin, they both find far more than they bargained for. This intuitive author just might have the answers Harrison's looking for, but will their newfound connection survive past the storm?

\* \* \*

"*W*here are your pages, Ivy?"

Ivy Blake winced at the snap of her agent's voice on the other end of the phone. Marianne was pulling out her stern, mom-of-three tone. That was never good. "They're coming."

At some theoretical, future time that was actually true.

"You've been saying that for weeks. And you've been avoiding me. You only do that when the words aren't flowing."

*You have no idea.*

"The book's been giving me a smidge of trouble." Understatement of the century. "But I promise, I'm nearly done." Flagrant lie. Ivy wondered if Marianne's Momdar was sounding an alarm. Ivy's own mama had an Eyebrow of Doom that could be heard over the phone when engaged.

"You have to give me something to give to Wally. I can't hold him off much longer."

Walter Caine—who inexplicably went by Wally, a fact that made it utterly impossible to take him seriously—was currently at the top of Ivy's avoid-at-all-costs list. Her editor was brilliant but a bit like a banty rooster when he got angry. He had deadlines. Of course, Ivy understood that. Everything about publishing involved deadlines. He'd absolutely blow a gasket if he knew she was still on Chapter One. The thirteenth version.

It was probably a sign.

"Next week." Was this what it felt like to be in debt to a bookie? Making absurd promises in hopes of avoiding broken kneecaps or cement shoes? Except in this case it was Ivy's career, not her actual life, in danger.

"Ivy." Marianne drew her name out to four syllables, which was tantamount to being middle-named by her mama.

Ivy hunched her shoulders. "I swear I'm finishing up the book. In fact, I'm taking a special trip for the express purpose of focusing on nothing but that until it's done."

Where the hell had that come from? She had no such plans. Apparently in lieu of offering up reasonable plot, her brain had decided to just spew spontaneous, bald-faced lies.

Her agent sighed. "Fine. How can I reach you?"

*In for a penny...*

"Oh, well, you can't. There's no internet up there, and I was warned that cell service is spotty. The cabin has absolute privacy and no distractions. It's perfect."

Actually, something like that *did* sound perfect. If she went totally off the grid, Marianne and Wally wouldn't know where to send the hitman when she missed her deadline. The one that had already been pushed back once.

*You've never missed a final deadline, and you're not going to start now.*

Marianne offered another beleaguered sigh. "Find an internet connection and check in on Monday or I'm hunting you down, understand?"

"Yes, ma'am." Ivy had no doubt she meant it. Despite her trio of children and the stable of other writers she managed, Marianne would absolutely get herself on a plane and show up on Ivy's doorstep if she thought it would get results.

"I'll do what I can to hold off Wally. This morning's starred review at Kirkus for *Hollow Point Ridge* should appease him for a little while. You know he loves nothing more than seeing you rack up acclaim."

"Because acclaim means dollar signs for us all," Ivy recited. As if she could forget that it was more than just her depending on income from her books.

"Damn straight. I forwarded the review to you. Check your email before you go," Marianne ordered.

She'd already seen the review this morning. Somebody had posted it in her fan group, which had generated a discussion thread that was already twenty pages deep about where she planned to go with the series next. But bringing that up would only prolong this conversation.

"Will do."

"Happy writing."

For just a moment, Ivy considered coming clean and telling Marianne the stark, unvarnished truth. Her agent was, ultimately, meant to be her advocate. But right now, she was only more pressure. So Ivy held in her snort of derision as she hung up the phone and tossed it on her desk.

It had been a long damned time since she'd been happy writing. The truth was, she had a raging case of writer's block, and she was already weeks past her initial deadline. That wasn't like her at all. She was a machine. Her first three books had poured out of her. The next three were each successively bigger, deeper, harder. And with each had come more success and higher expectations from her publisher, who wanted to capitalize on momentum to maximize sales. That was a business decision on their part. She was a commodity. Ivy understood that. And up to now, she'd been able to work with it.

But along with the professional pressures had come the rabid excitement of her fans. They loved the world she created, the characters she'd given them, and not a day went by when she didn't get emails and messages on social media demanding to know when the next book was coming because OMG they needed it yesterday! They had no idea the months, sometimes years of work that went into each book. What ate up her entire life occupied theirs for mere hours or days. And their insatiable enthusiasm was just one more stone piling on and crushing her with stress.

This book wasn't like the other six in her best-selling series, and she just hadn't found the right hook yet.

She would. Of course, she would. She just needed some more time and less pressure.

"Why don't you ask for world peace, while you're at it?"

Dropping into her office chair, Ivy shoved back from the desk and rolled across her office to the massive whiteboard occupying one wall. At this stage, the whole surface should've been covered with color-coded sticky notes detailing the assorted character arcs and how they drove and were driven by the action of the external plot. But it was empty other than the scrawl of "Michael" at the top in red marker. Below it a bright yellow note read, *You are a stubborn, taciturn asshole, who won't talk to me.* In a fit of pique and stress cleaning earlier in the week, she'd stripped away version number twelve of her plot. Now she couldn't face the blank space.

Page fright was so much a real thing.

Maybe she *should* get away. Find one of those out-of-the-way cabins to rent, with no phone, no internet, no way to be crushed under the weight of other people's expectations. Maybe then she could hear herself think.

Rolling back to her computer, she opened a browser, compulsively clicking on the little envelope that told her she had seventy-nine unread messages.

She'd cleared her inbox this morning.

"Why do I do this to myself?"

She started to close it out when a subject line caught her attention.

*Come visit the brand new spa at The Misfit Inn!*

She'd forgotten about The Misfit Inn. Last summer, she and several girlfriends had taken a weekend trip up there in spontaneous celebration of Deanna's divorce. The owners had mentioned they were considering adding a spa. Ivy had signed up for the mailing list and promptly forgotten about it. She opened the email, feeling the first hints of excitement as she read it. Okay, maybe that was desperation. But really? A spa? One set right in the gorgeous Smoky Mountains, just four short hours away? She desperately needed to relax. It had to be a sign from the Universe.

Someone answered on the second ring. "Thank you for calling The Misfit Inn. This is Pru. How can I help you?"

Ivy remembered Pru, the kind-hearted woman who'd done everything possible to make the inn feel like home.

"This is Ivy Blake. I don't know if you remember me, but a bunch of girlfriends and I stayed with y'all last summer for a Thank God I'm Divorced party weekend—"

"Deanna's group! Yes, certainly we remember y'all."

"Well, I got the email about the opening of the spa, and it did say call to ask about booking specials that covered the inn and spa, so here I am."

"Wonderful!" The genuine warmth in Pru's voice had some of the knots relaxing. "How many?"

"Just me."

"In need of some pampering?"

"You have no idea."

"Okay then. When were you wanting to come?"

The sooner the better. "Um…today?"

"Today! Good gracious. Y'all are all about the spontaneity aren't you?"

*Sure, let's call it that.* "I know it's last-minute, but I was hoping to book two weeks."

"We can certainly accommodate that. But you should know before you make the drive that we're supposed to be having some really serious winter weather. Full-on snow and ice. The drive is liable to be pretty nasty and there's a really good chance you could get snowed in."

Snowed in at an inn and spa for two weeks, far away from

everyone who knew her? "That sounds absolutely perfect. I'll see you in a few hours."

\* \* \*

GRIEF SMELLED OF ONIONS, cheese, and cream of something soup. Multiple tables groaned under the weight of death casseroles along one wall of the church fellowship hall. The scent of it wafted over as Harrison Wilkes walked in, simultaneously curdling his stomach and making it growl. A quick scan of the room told him the widow hadn't made it over from the cemetery yet, but he spotted the man he'd come to support hovering near the dessert table. Careful not to make eye contact with the other mourners, Harrison wove his way through the crowd.

If possible, Ty looked worse than he had during the service. But then, he was here against medical advice and had served as a pall bearer. Sweat beaded along his brow. His shoulder had to be hurting like a son of a bitch from over-exertion.

"Sit your ass down before you fall down, Brooks."

Ty lifted bloodshot eyes to Harrison's. "You're not my CO."

"I'm still your friend." He took a step closer and lowered his voice. "You did your duty to Garrett. Don't you go blowing all the work you've done in PT by pushing yourself too far."

Ty's pale face turned mulish, but before he could pop off, another familiar voice interrupted.

"Step aside, y'all. I've got food to add to the table."

Sebastian Donnelly muscled his way past, a casserole dish in hand. Its contents smelled both familiar and noxious.

"Tell me that's not what I think it is," Harrison said.

Sebastian plunked the dish down on the table and took off the foil. "My famous barbeque beef casserole."

"More like infamous," Ty said. "Only you would try to make a casserole out of MREs."

"I tried to talk him out of it." Porter Ingram joined the group. "We all know how much Garrett hated that shit."

Sebastian straightened, suddenly sober. "Yeah, but he'd hate this damned wake even more."

They all lapsed into silence, aware of the dubious privilege of standing here able to bitch and moan about the wake. A privilege Garrett didn't have.

Everything about this sucked. Funerals sucked to begin with, no matter who they were for. They sucked worse when it was a friend. Someone you'd fought alongside, who'd saved your ass, who should've made it home. And they sucked most when they brought up old shit you were still trying to move past. There were too many ghosts stirred up for anybody to be comfortable.

"Come on. Let's either make plates or go sit down." Porter's voice interrupted Harrison's thoughts.

"I'm not hungry," Ty insisted.

"Then let's get out of the way for the people who are." Porter smoothly managed to nudge him toward a table.

"Always the peacemaker," Harrison murmured.

"Yeah, he's good at that." Sebastian picked up a paper plate and began filling it from the assortment of dishes, skipping his own offering to the spread.

Not knowing what else to do, Harrison fell in behind him.

"How are you doing with all this?" Sebastian asked.

It was instinct to deflect. "Better than Ty."

They both looked across the room, where he'd finally sat, shoulders bowed, head bent as if he couldn't hold it up anymore. Porter had a chair pulled up, talking to him in a low voice, one hand on his arm.

Sebastian scooped up some kind of hash brown casserole. "You think he'll come back from this?"

"You never come back from this. Not really." Harrison twitched his shoulders inside the jacket of his suit, wishing the thing didn't feel like a straitjacket.

Glancing at Ty, seeing the clench of his jaw, the lines of strain fanning out from his eyes, Harrison knew exactly the kind of shit going through his buddy's head. He'd been there. It was the reason he'd left the Army. It didn't feel like three years. Not when so many familiar faces filled the room. Men he'd fought with, bled with. Many were still fighting the fight. In his own way, so was he. But he couldn't do what they did. Not anymore.

Harrison trailed Sebastian across the room, nodding acknowledgments to those who greeted him, but not stopping until he reached Ty's table. Ty went silent, straightening in his chair with a Styrofoam cup he no doubt wished held something stronger than sweet tea, as they all realized Bethany Reeves had just arrived.

Ty hadn't spoken to her at the funeral. He hadn't even been able to go near her. He blamed himself for Garrett's death. Wrongly. But none of them could talk him out of that at this stage. So the three of them ranged around him, buffers between their friend and everybody else here. They shoveled in food and talked football and other stupid, civilian shit because he needed distraction and it was all they could do here. But they each tracked Bethany's progress around the room and braced themselves when she made her way to Ty.

He didn't bolt. Ty was no coward and his mother had raised him better than that. But Harrison knew he wanted to.

Bethany's face was ravaged by grief as she reached out for Ty's hand. "Ty."

"Ma'am."

Her expression twisted. "Don't you ma'am me, Tyson Brooks. You were the closest thing Garrett had to a brother, and that makes you family."

Ty's Adam's apple bobbed. "I loved him like a brother."

"I know you did." She tried to smile, but tears streamed down her face. "He got out because of you. You're a hero for that."

Ty shoved to his feet so fast his chair tipped over, the metal clattering against the industrial tile floor as he jerked his hand from Bethany's. In the sudden silence, his words sounded too loud. "I'm no hero."

He walked out without another word. With apologetic looks at Bethany, Sebastian and Porter followed, no doubt to make sure he didn't do something stupid. That left Harrison to find the right thing to say to the poor woman to smooth things over. Fuck.

He didn't know how much Bethany knew about the details of her husband's death. Some of the details were classified, as Ranger missions often were. There were things he didn't know himself, but could easily fill in from experience. And he knew those things wouldn't bring comfort to Garrett's widow. In truth, he had no idea how to comfort those left behind. Standing beside her, looking into her stricken face, he felt all the old impotence rise up, strong enough to choke him.

Harrison didn't know what he said to Bethany. His head was too full of the visits he'd had to make to the significant others of his own men. But he said something, taking a moment to squeeze her hand because even he could tell she needed human connection. The grasp of her cold, clammy fingers sent him back, until his head echoed with tears and recriminations. Needing to get the hell out, he made his excuses and all but ran for the exit.

Outside the fellowship hall, he braced his hands against the trunk of a car and sucked in big, cleansing lungfuls of the cold, winter air. It was so cold it hurt, colder than it should be in north Georgia this time of year. But the pain was good. The pain brought him back to the now.

"Hey."

Harrison straightened and turned to Porter. "Where's Ty?"

"Sebastian took him home. He's gonna stick around a while, keep an eye on him."

"Good." Ty didn't need to be left alone right now. He had a long, dark road ahead.

Porter angled his head, studying Harrison with eyes that saw too much. "You're not looking so great."

Because it was Porter, because he'd see through the bullshit, Harrison admitted the truth. "I need to get the hell out of here."

"I've got a cabin nobody's using. It's a chunk out from town, away from everything and everybody. It's yours if you want it. Peace and quiet and a chance to get your head screwed on straight. And Eden's Ridge is closer than you driving all the way home."

The whole idea of being in the middle of nowhere in the mountains of Tennessee, away from people and pressures, where he could *think* was beyond appealing. He had some decisions to make. It would be easier to make them without all the reminders of the past.

"Lead the way."

Get your copy of *Baby It's Cold Outside today!*

# OTHER BOOKS BY KAIT NOLAN

**A complete and up-to-date list of all my books can be found at https://kaitnolan.com.**

\* \* \*

### THE MISFIT INN SERIES
### SMALL TOWN FAMILY ROMANCE

- *When You Got A Good Thing* (Kennedy and Xander)
- *Til There Was You* (Misty and Denver)
- *Those Sweet Words* (Pru and Flynn)
- *Stay A Little Longer* (Athena and Logan)
- *Bring It On Home* (Maggie and Porter)

### RESCUE MY HEART SERIES
### SMALL TOWN MILITARY ROMANCE

- *Baby It's Cold Outside* (Ivy and Harrison)
- *What I Like About You* (Laurel and Sebastian)

## WISHFUL SERIES
## SMALL TOWN SOUTHERN ROMANCE

- *Once Upon A Coffee* (Avery and Dillon)
- *To Get Me To You* (Cam and Norah)
- *Know Me Well* (Liam and Riley)
- *Be Careful, It's My Heart* (Brody and Tyler)
- *Just For This Moment* (Myles and Piper)
- *Wish I Might* (Reed and Cecily)
- *Turn My World Around* (Tucker and Corinne)
- *Dance Me A Dream* (Jace and Tara)
- *See You Again* (Trey and Sandy)
- *The Christmas Fountain* (Chad and Mary Alice)
- *You Were Meant For Me* (Mitch and Tess)
- *A Lot Like Christmas* (Ryan and Hannah)
- *Dancing Away With My Heart* (Zach and Lexi)

## WISHING FOR A HERO SERIES (A WISHFUL SPINOFF SERIES)
## SMALL TOWN ROMANTIC SUSPENSE

- *Make You Feel My Love* (Judd and Autumn)
- *Watch Over Me* (Nash and Rowan)
- *Can't Take My Eyes Off You* (Ethan and Miranda)
- *Burn For You* (Sean and Delaney)

## MEET CUTE ROMANCE
## SMALL TOWN SHORT ROMANCE

- *Once Upon A Snow Day*
- *Once Upon A New Year's Eve*
- *Once Upon An Heirloom*
- *Once Upon A Coffee*
- *Once Upon A Campfire*
- *Once Upon A Rescue*

## SUMMER CAMP
## CONTEMPORARY ROMANCE

- *Once Upon A Campfire*
- *Second Chance Summer*

# ABOUT KAIT

Kait is a Mississippi native, who often swears like a sailor, calls everyone sugar, honey, or darlin', and can wield a bless your heart like a saber or a Snuggie, depending on requirements.

You can find more information on this RITA ® Award-winning author and her books on her website http://kaitnolan.com. While you're there, sign up for her newsletter so you don't miss out on news about new releases: https://kaitnolan.com/newsletter/

CPSIA information can be obtained
at www.ICGtesting.com
Printed in the USA
LVHW051247070121
675556LV00003B/249

9 781648 351198